D0597201

String
Music

String Music

Rick Telander

Cricket Books

A Marcato Book

Chicago

Text copyright © 2002 by Rick Telander
All rights reserved
Printed in the United States of America
Designed by Anthony Jacobson
Third printing, 2002

Library of Congress Cataloging-in-Publication Data

Telander, Rick.
  String music / Rick Telander.— 1st ed.
      p. cm.
Summary: An unlikely friendship develops between a lonely
eleven-year-old boy and the professional basketball star whom he
idolizes.
  ISBN 0-8126-2657-5 (Cloth : alk. paper)
  [1. Basketball—Fiction. 2. Friendship—Fiction. 3. Family
problems—Fiction. 4. Schools—Fiction.] I. Title.
  PZ7.T235 St 2002
  [Fic]—dc21
                                                    2002000600

For Lauren, Cary, Robin, and Zack

My Fort

THEY WERE AT IT AGAIN, so I got out of there.

I'm eleven and nobody notices you when you're eleven. It's not like being eight, when you're maybe going to fall into a hole, or fifteen, when you're pretty much an adult. Eleven is nothing.

It wasn't too cold out, but I grabbed my jacket from the hook by the front door and put it on because it can be a little chilly in the fort, and anyway, a jacket is a handy thing to have no matter what.

As I walked into the trees and down the hill, I could still hear them arguing. Yak, yak, yakking at each other. My mom was mad about something, and Lulu was yelling back real loud. You this and you that. A lot of screeching. Lulu is sixteen but you'd think she was thirty, because she knows everything. My mom gets irritated a lot with her. I heard a door slam and

1

something crash, and then I was around the bend where the path sort of splits apart.

If the trail looks too straight or obvious, I'll get a bunch of leaves and spread them around or I'll find some sticks and put them down in a careful but random way, like how they might have fallen if there were no kid around at all and you wouldn't think about walking there. I don't want somebody finding the fort. Never. And I sure don't want anybody finding it because they just followed a trail right up to the front door and said, "Hey look, a fort," when all they were doing was walking in the woods down a path, looking at nature.

So you can't see my path. But I know where it is. It's everywhere and it's nowhere. I can find it in the dark. There's an oak tree and then four shiny trees with names I don't know right almost in a row. Then there are a bunch of sticker bushes that you can go around, or through in the special way I know. Then there is a mulberry bush and seven baby hemlocks and a bunch of lilies of the valley and a place where toadstools grow after a rain, and a big vine connected to a maple tree, just hanging like a real thick snake. There is the swampy part where water comes right out of the hill and makes everything muddy and where I know never to leave footprints. And there is more.

My fort is a cave in the side of the gully about ten feet up the hill from the creek. It's really not a cave, either, but more of a big round hole around an old dead tree. It goes back about six feet and there are roots hanging around and you can't stand up straight. But I found it when I was ten, and I fixed it up and made it so nobody else would ever find it, and I don't care what anybody thinks.

My Fort

I crawled under the log in front, looking to make sure nobody was around, which is what I always do. I looked at the canvas door. It was okay. The leaves and mud and sticks were holding to it fine. I went inside.

Inside it was real dark like it always is for a few seconds. Maybe even darker than usual because now it was dusk and the trees kept a lot of light from even making it down this far, due to their leaves, which are fairly thick.

I kept my eyes closed tight for a couple seconds, which is something I do as an experiment. If it's black, then how can it be darker with your eyes closed than with them open? I don't know, but it is. I find that funny, and so I usually do it.

After a while I turned on the flashlight that was hanging from a string. *Foom!* I could see for a second, then I went blind. Then slowly my vision came back. It was all nice and cozy. A nice light in this little place of mine. Everything dry. Safe.

There was my pillow. There was the candle. I reached behind the big root number three and got the stick matches I have in a small bundle with a rubber band holding them tight. I took one and scratched it on the match-striking rock I got down at the creek where it bends around way down by the McMahons' house.

Fwish. It lit right up with a nice yellow-and-blue flame and a sound and smell like the bottle rockets I can get from my friend Clement when he and his parents go to South Carolina and come back with stuff like that. I held the match real careful until the flame was calm and orange, and then I lit my candle. Now there were two shadows of everything on the walls of the fort, and it was nice.

There was my table. It's just a foot off the ground, but that's okay when you're basically sitting on the ground all the time, anyway. The army guys were kneeling in place, holding their bazookas. I turned one of them toward the door in case an enemy tried to break in.

"You have permission to fire at will, corporal," I said.

My twigs were there and so were the wildflowers in the vase, though they were pretty wilted just since yesterday, and my compass and my favorite books, *White Fang* and *All about Stars* and *The Year of the Turtle* and the dictionary.

I crawled in a little farther and looked for Solomon in his terrarium. He was buried under some leafy stuff, but I could see his nose. I reached in and pulled him out, and he was real black, with those bright yellow spots and overall just as shiny as licorice. He was only a salamander but he was my pal, and I didn't like thinking about letting him go in a few weeks, which I had to do so he could hibernate for winter.

I looked for Flossie and she was there, too, at the edge of her web, just sitting. She is a very fat spider with a brownish body and mostly brown legs, and I had to read up on her to see what she was going to do when everything froze and if she was real poisonous, which she is not.

Animals are my friends and I want to be nice to them and I want to keep them around, too. Knowing what to do with animals is hard because you never can be sure what they're thinking. But if you try to think like you would if you were very small and ate strange things and had no clothes, I think it's a start.

I slid to the back of the fort. I unrolled the rubber mat and put the big carpet square on top of it, and I sat there.

"The General has need of information. Is there a report from the front lines?"

All quiet, sir.

"And the turrets?"

Negative, sir.

The army guys went back to their stations.

I leaned back and looked at my poster of Jasper Jasmine. He's only the best basketball player in the world. He was flying like a bird, holding the ball like a rolled-up sock. He must have hands that could wrap around my head. He is *so* good. I grabbed my little foam ball and started shooting at the plastic basket I had nailed to root five. I have a couple more pictures of Jasper Jasmine hanging around. Nice ones from *Sports Illustrated* and even a black-and-white one from the paper that shows him getting ready to shoot a free throw, with sweat coming off his chin—*drip, drip, drip.*

I stopped shooting for a minute and took some gumdrops out of the bag hanging from root two. They were still fine. Then I started shooting some more. I tried to see if I could get the ball to roll back to me so I didn't have to move anything but my right arm. When I could get that to happen, it was pretty cool. I got into a rhythm. One, two, three, four in a row. Then a miss. Then some bank shots.

Jasmine drives, he backs out, he shakes his man, he hits from midcourt.

Why wasn't basketball this easy for me? Why was I this little, kind-of-nobody guy? There are so many people in the world. And I was barely one of them. I was like a minus sign. A zero.

I knew I had to go back soon because even my mom would get concerned if I just vanished. Like, *poof,* vaporized or something. Even if she and Lulu fought all night. Maybe not right away, but sooner or later she'd notice, like when she realized nobody had taken out the garbage. Sometimes I wonder if Mom even thinks about me at all except as an annoying boy eating her food and sleeping down the hall.

I faked like I was dribbling. I passed to Jasper Jasmine. *Shoot it! Let it fly!* And I pretended I was him, and I did shoot it and it went smooth off my fingers and through the air and off the glass and through the net, and I stopped then because I needed to get back and because I was crying. I was crying pretty hard all of a sudden. That'll happen sometimes. At least it does to me. But I don't think anybody needs to know.

II
Practice

"WHAT ARE YOU DOING, Dimwit!" Mr. Raltney yelled.

My last name is Denwood, and so Mr. Raltney thinks it's funny to call me Dimwit, which I've heard only a million times from people in my life, and from just about everybody who thinks they're clever and real original.

I shook my head because I didn't really know.

"You mean you don't know, or are you telling me you don't want to tell me how dumb that move was?"

He said *dumb* like he had a lemon stuck in his mouth, and the word was hard for him to get out. He even pronounced the *b* at the end so it went *dum-bah*.

"Well, uh—"

He blew his whistle loud.

7

"Quiet!" he roared. "Dimwit, there's a reason you're last man on this team. Why do you think that is?"

The other players looked at me. At least, I think they did, because I was looking down at this point.

I could tell some of them were embarrassed and some were excited, because when somebody gets screamed at and really made fun of, it is pathetic and exciting at the same time. But I didn't like it. I thought about my fort. I thought about Solomon all black and shiny.

". . . because you don't do what I say," he was saying. "Gimme ten laps, and after one, I want the whole team to join in. Then maybe you'll get the point."

"Thanks, stupid," said Vance Lester almost in my ear as we ran. He was a star on our fifth-grade team. He played almost every minute of every game, and his dad took videos of all of it, even including when we did warmups. What could I say to Vance? I couldn't say anything.

When we were done, I kneeled on the sideline while the team ran rebounding drills. I was pretty much the extra man. But I counted my blessings. At least I was on the team. Of course, our school is small, so only eleven guys went out for the team, and I was eleven. We don't even have a football team and we start basketball early and play other small schools that don't have football teams, either. They have a rule at our school that you can't cut anybody unless the coach runs out of uniforms. But I think he's got fifteen. I'm pretty sure he's got four more uniforms as spares, and anyway, since I started school, as a little kid, I don't think there ever have been more guys than uniforms. So nobody gets cut. Not even me.

I knelt and watched the other players do a scrimmage. I watched with what looked like great interest, but I was really back in my fort. I was there holding Solomon, and we were talking.

We should go check the turrets, Robby.

Agreed, Sol, let me get my crossbow. Do you have your broadsword?

Right here, master. If an ogre comes at us, he'll feel cold steel, I assure you.

Flossie, man the main gate.

Aye, aye, sir.

Mr. Raltney was there beside me. He was talking to me, but he wasn't.

"The zone press will give us trouble," he said. "See that! Look for the outlet. *Boom*, right now! You give the ball to an athlete like Lester, and he'll make it happen."

Mr. Raltney blew his whistle. He called everybody to center court. "Take her in," he hollered. "Acorn Hills on Wednesday. Make sure you have rides. Dimwit, you and Miles rack the balls."

I didn't mind that. I liked racking the balls. I dribbled each one and fired it into the rack, getting the rebound and firing again until the ball stayed where it belonged. The feel of the leather on my hands was worth being the last guy into the locker room. I wasn't going to take a shower, anyway. No way. You have to be a solid part of the team before you do that. Like I said, I was eleven out of eleven. And I was eleven years old. It all kind of fit.

* * *

Some of us stood out on the big steps that go down from the front of the school. It wasn't real dark out, but it was getting there. The guys' moms or dads honked, and then the kid would run off to whatever car it was. Sometimes, like with Billy McReynolds and Luke Delgato and Chump Ernst, they all got in together because they had a car pool. Me and Kenny Koski sat down. After a while we were the only ones left.

My mom said she'd come by to pick me up, but I was wondering if she forgot. She has a lot on her mind these days now that Dad's gone and she's really busy. So I know it's easy to forget things. I mean, I forget stuff constantly. She's not crazy about basketball, either. She told me I was silly for playing, and she's probably right. But I'm kind of a bad person in that I really am not very good at anything. Still, I just had this itch to play basketball. I figured I could always grow like sixteen inches, suddenly, and then what if I wasn't on the team? That would be a mistake. A giant tall guy like me just walking around? I might just shoot up one day. Stranger things have happened.

"You like macaroni?" asked Kenny.

"Sorta. You?"

Kenny shrugged. "Does it take a long time to cook?"

"Kind of in the middle, I think," I said.

"'Cause that's what we're having for dinner. Mom said. A guy gets tired of waiting, you know, Rob?"

I did. So I pulled out my miniature basketball from my backpack. I bounced it in front of me, then let Kenny dribble it. It was hard to do, but not too hard. We started playing a game, shooting over each other at the railings on either side of the steps. I was ahead, ten to eight, when Kenny's mom came.

Practice

"Need a ride, Rob?" she asked, leaning over Kenny's little snotty-nosed brother who was crunched up in the front seat and wailing about something or other.

"No thanks, Mrs. Koski. Mom'll be here in"—I looked at my watch—"three minutes. Thanks."

A teacher came out after a while. Her heels clicked down the sidewalk. All the team was gone. It was kind of dark. Practice had been over for more than an hour. Actually, it was plain dark. I saw Mr. Hoodin, the janitor, moving down the hallway with a mop. Another teacher came out and looked at me a little funny, like what the heck was I doing there. I think she was from second grade.

Mom is really busy lately. She's depressed sometimes, and sometimes she's just mad. She's always got a million things to get done.

Because of my journeys to my fort, I've learned not to be too afraid of the dark, so I picked up my stuff and zipped my jacket. I walked down the sidewalk and out toward the main road. It really wasn't a bad night for going home on your own.

III

School

I DON'T KNOW, but if I had a choice, I'd be really stuck trying to figure out which class I like the least. You compare geography and math and science and social studies, and you've got a real contest in my opinion. I do like English, though. But only when we read books or short stories like the one we read about a man in Africa who has a battle with these army ants. It was awesome. They pretty much marched through everything that was in their way like a herd of buffalo until the man had this moat filled with gasoline and he lit it with a match, and I guess you can figure out what happened after that. But I'll tell you, history is right up there with the most boring stuff ever invented.

Today we were talking about French people, all the kings and ladies, like Marie Antoinette, and rebellion and poor people with pitchforks, and fancy people in slippers and tights. Mrs. Versheen gave us some time to read a chapter about some stuff that had to do with France's problem with some confused English lords. I opened my book, but I got bored in a sentence or two. I knew that was going to happen. So I went to my remedy.

The girl who sits behind me has red hair, and her name is Kathy Amblee. She gets teased a lot because of her hair—Kathy Carrot and stuff like that—but I don't mind red hair. I told her one time that she was as cool as Red Auerbach, who used to coach the Celtics. She had no idea who he was, but she was my friend after that. So I asked her if she would scratch my back. She wasn't real hot on the idea. But I explained how easy it was to do—just stretch her arm out across her desk, hold a pen with the top on and rub it slowly across my back where it sticks up above my chair. Not hard, and be careful Mrs. Versheen can't see. And since I'm kind of bony, she had to watch out for my neck bone and those shoulder things that stick out. I told her how important it would be to me.

At first Kathy only did it a couple times. Then I eased her into doing it more. I called her Coach Auerbach, and she liked that. By October she would do it just about whenever I asked her, and she could read and do her own stuff and hardly even think about the fact she was doing it. But I loved it. It relaxed me. It made all that boring stuff practically vanish. And what I would do to make things even better is I would hide a paper behind my raised history book, get out my four-colored pen, and draw basketball pictures.

I was working on one of Jasper Jasmine speeding past a rocket ship in outer space, smiling as he blew past that slow piece of junk, when I felt Kathy stop rubbing with her pen.

That broke my concentration, and I started to turn around to tell her she wasn't done yet. That's when I saw a big ugly face staring into my eyeballs.

"Ah, we are so smart, we have decided to become an artist," said Mrs. Versheen. "*Merci.* Documenting the French Revolution?"

She had snuck up on me while I was working on the label on the ball that Jasper Jasmine was palming. It was, like, jet-propelling him past the rocket ship into outer space, the ball was. And it was going to have blue flames coming off it. She snatched my drawing away and held it up like a stinky sock.

"Look at this. Our artist has documented history."

She made sure everybody could see that there wasn't much French about my work, and then she crumpled it slowly into a wad and dropped it on the floor. Oh boy. This was disaster.

She told me to go sit outside the room, by the coat hangers along the wall. "You're not needed in this classroom," she said. She said my next step after that if I wasn't careful would be down to Mr. Romine's office and then out the door. Mr. Romine was the principal. This was not a good day for me overall. In fact, it was a bad day. But when you got down to it, it was just one of many.

IV
Acorn Hills

I MADE IT TO the game with everybody else. Larry Wheeling, the manager, this kind of funny little guy with one ear that lies flat on his head and the other that sticks out like a pull tab, said it was okay for me to ride with his mom and his two sisters in their station wagon.

All of the guys put on their uniforms in the locker room, but I had some spare time because I was wearing mine under my clothes. While guys were changing, I walked around looking at stuff. I went to the end of the lockers and then down a hall. I found this door that was partway open, so I opened it all the way and turned on the light. It was cool because it was an equipment closet with lots of sports stuff in it. There were practice jerseys and soccer balls and those orange cones you use in gym class for shuttle runs and stuff. There was an electric air pump and two old footballs, a bunch of broomsticks, a tether ball, five red playground balls, some plastic hockey pucks, a bag full of bats, down markers, adhesive tape, a nail with whistles hanging from it, a couple of those stupid black ref hats, a couple of flat old basketballs, and one rack with two layers of good, really sweet, shoot-around basketballs.

I picked up a ball and let my fingers feel the pebbles on it and the lines and the little dot where you stuck in the air needle. How do you make something round? I mean perfectly round? That's always been a big question I've had. I put the ball back and then ran my hands over the other ones on the top row. I remembered reading a story about the man who invented basketball a long time ago and how he was figuring the game wouldn't last. Or at least he wasn't sure. Like a hundred years ago or more. I remembered his name was something Naismith. A cool name. But I mean, he couldn't tell how awesome his game was?

On the floor there was a box full of cans of powdered stickum. I pulled one out and shook a bunch of the yellow dust on first one hand, then the other. I just kept sprinkling it on, and then I got too much in the air because I started coughing and hacking with all the little particles floating around.

"Hey!" said a man. "What are you doing in there?"

"Nothing," I said, staggering out. Then I coughed some more and my eyes were watering and I was a mess. *Hack-hack.*

"Are you from Central?" said the man, waving his arms in the air, trying to clear it up a little bit.

I nodded. Because I couldn't speak.

"Well, get out of here and get back to your team, understand me?"

I nodded and I went back down the hall to our locker, coughing all the way. My throat tasted like a pine tree. The team was just filing out onto the floor, so I followed behind.

"You sick?" asked Dickie Miles.

I shook my head. "Sticky," I wheezed.

He looked at me weird. But I was coughing again, so I couldn't say anything.

In the lay-up line I took a pass, and man, the ball almost stuck on my palms like a Velcro patch. It was so ridiculous. It was awesome. But then I tried to shoot, and the ball went off sideways because I could barely let it go.

"You're pathetic," whispered Vance as he went by me with this really fake grin. "Double-ace pathetic ding-a-ling."

The game was a good one. Of course I didn't get in. But I had a great view when anything happened. My coughing vanished entirely by the second quarter, but I drank so much water to kill the pine taste that Larry Wheeling said, "Jeez, Dim, save some for the fish."

At halftime I felt a little sick, like I was waterlogged, but I went to the bathroom for about five minutes, and Larry gave me some gum and that made me fine.

I got to warm up in the lay-up line with everybody before the third quarter started, and I made three lay-ups in a row. On the fourth one the ball rolled around and I don't know if it went in, because I had my head looking backwards and I crashed into Chump Ernst, and whoa, I went flying.

"Dude, you're gonna kill somebody" was all Chump said. Mr. Raltney was over at the scorers' table, so he didn't see.

I sat quietly on the bench and watched the game. We won because Vance Lester was lighting it up. He is smooth on the floor in a way I'll never be. I could hear his old man yelling, "Do it, Vance," when he wasn't looking through his video camera. I got excited, too, and by the very end, I was cheering hard for our team.

I felt pretty good because of my successful warmup shots, and then Mr. Raltney said, "Dimwit, rack 'em up." And I put the balls in the right places, which I loved, and it wasn't too bad a day at all.

V

The Mall

ON SATURDAY my mind was wandering. I was riding my
bike and I stopped on the sidewalk of this small bridge that
goes over a mostly dry creek and I was looking down at the
leaves as they landed in the main puddle. No matter how little
the leaves were, when they hit the water, they sent out circles
that moved like perfect basketballs all the way to the dirt
shore.

I was really concentrating, and then somebody said, "Hi,
Robby." It was Kathy Amblee, old Coach Auerbach, and she
was stopped on her bike right next to me. I must have
jumped ten feet when she said my name, because I was so
interested in the circles, and I guess I yelled, too, because
Kathy screamed, and man, it was all pretty crazy for a second.

"Oh, gee, you scared me," she said.

"Sorry," I said. "You scared me, too."

We laughed, and then we talked about nothing in particular.

I pointed out the leaf circles, and she said, "Oh, yeah," but I could tell she wasn't as interested as I was. I thought it would be radical to drop a firecracker in the mud from up here and see what kind of a hole it would make. I told Kathy that, and she wrinkled her nose. We'd talked about fire-crackers before, so I knew she wasn't very excited about them. She knew my friend Clement, who sometimes got me firecrackers from down south, and I told her I hadn't seen him in a long time. He went to a school Kathy went to before she moved closer to Central.

"Didn't you know?" she said.

"Know what?"

"He moved."

"Where?"

"I think South Carolina. His dad lost his job or something."

"You sure?"

"I know he's gone. I just rode past his house and it's empty, and there's a sign up."

Since there was nothing else going on, I said why didn't we ride somewhere. I wouldn't normally hang out with a girl, but Kathy wasn't a basic girl in a lot of ways. She had that red hair and she didn't say much and she wasn't snotty. She was kind of boring, I guess, but not in a bad way. She was okay. Plus, I kind of owed her for all the times she'd scratched my back.

"You want to go to the mall?" I asked.

She said sure, and we rode there by the back way so we didn't have to go on any big roads. We parked our bikes and walked past the huge water fountain and in through the big glass doors. We got sodas at a stand and then walked around looking at stuff. All of a sudden I saw a group of guys from school up on the second floor, and I thought maybe we should turn around and go the other way.

But Luke Delgato saw me, and he said, "Hey man, come on up. We're gonna get some food. Come on, Rob."

I looked at Kathy. "You want to go see the guys?" I asked.

"Not really."

I understood why she wouldn't.

"You don't mind if I go, do you?" I said.

"No, that's okay. Go ahead."

She didn't say it like she really meant it.

"That was fun riding with you, Kathy. I'll see you in school on Monday. Okay?"

"Sure, Robby. See ya."

I smiled at her, and then I sprinted up the escalator and caught up with Luke.

We joined the guys, and all of us started eating burgers in the food court. Emil Wingate, a really skinny guy with a cowlick on each side of his head and a braided necklace around his skinny neck, started shooting spitballs at fat ladies when they went by. I have to admit it was funny to see them jump and look around, and Emil sitting there so innocent like he was reading a magazine and just minding his own business. But then one lady with stretchy flowered pants started coming over to us, and we all bolted before she could start ragging at our butts. When we got together again up on the third floor, way past the escalator, we wandered around not doing much.

"Rob, you got a dad?" Luke Delgato asked me.

I told him sure I had a dad, but he just wasn't around because he was in Texas where there was opportunity.

"Your folks, like, divorced?"

We were looking in the window of a fingernail polish store, which was retarded.

"Yeah," I said.

But what I didn't say was that they were more like split up and mad, because they weren't divorced, just apart, and Dad had vanished to Texas, and he didn't care about any of us or anything except his own selfish self. Well, that's what Mom said. It had been almost two years since he left, and Mom was a mess over it. She said Dad was so inconsiderate, he was a pig, but I still remembered him nailing up my basket over the garage at home and calling me Champ. It was a long time ago, though. Two years can be most of your life if you're not that old.

We went into a sporting goods store and started messing with the balls and shoes. The guy who was working there didn't like us, and he came over and stood right by us and said, "Do you want to buy something or not, because if you're just hanging around, I'm going to ask you to leave."

We left and when we got outside, Emil said that guy was a jerk. Then he pulled a pair of socks from under his shirt.

"Did you swipe those?" somebody asked.

"Yep," said Emil. And he had a big dopey grin on his skinny face.

We rode down an escalator to the second floor, and Emil rolled the socks into a ball and heaved them halfway to the other side of the mall. Then we went into another store, and a couple of the guys started taking one shoe at a time from this big rack of mostly skateboard shoes out near the front and sticking them real slowly under their shirts. It was making me nervous. They looked demented with these shoes out-lined in their clothes, but they kept doing it, one guy at a time putting a shoe under his shirt.

"Come on Dimnuts," whispered this other kid, Stevie. "Get some."

I looked around, then I picked up a shoe. It looked like it was about my size. But there was only one. This was crazy. There weren't two of any of the shoes. What could you do with one shoe? Maybe if you had one leg or something.

And something else bothered me. I remembered Mrs. Sanderson, in the first grade, when she said if you take some-thing that isn't yours, no matter how little or dumb, it's stealing. Even when I took a cookie from my obnoxious sister, I kind of felt bad because Mrs. Sanderson always seemed to be floating around saying, "Now, now, that's stealing."

All of a sudden the guys were walking away real fast and I was just standing there like a pole. I couldn't tell, but it looked like they all took some stuff, or at least most of them did. As I watched them go down the hallway and past more stores and then down another escalator, I don't know why, but I just stood there. A store guy looked at the shoe racks, then out into the mall, then at the shoe racks again. Then I walked in the other direction.

When I went outside, all the guys' bikes were gone, which I figured they would be. Kathy's was gone, too. I undid my chain, got on my bike, and rode back home. I just didn't feel like doing any more stuff with anybody. I had enough trouble in my life without getting in trouble for taking dumb old shoes. It seemed like lately there was trouble everywhere.

I parked my bike by the tree near our mailbox, I got my basketball from inside the garage, and start shooting baskets.

Mom's car wasn't in the garage, so I guessed she was gone some place. And if Lulu was around, I couldn't tell. One time I asked her to shoot some hoops with me, and all she did was put her finger in her mouth and do like this fake gagging thing and say, "Fer sure."

So I shot by myself. I was Jasper Jasmine in game seven of the NBA finals. The Thunder was down by two and the clock was ticking away and Jasmine had the ball way outside with three men on him. Five . . . four . . . three . . . two . . . Jasmine shot from fifty feet, and the ball just flew up into the Thunder Dome's lights, and then it came sailing down through all this smoke and . . . and . . . hit nothing but total net. Twine time. Pure string music.

Thunder wins! Thunder wins!

I got the ball back and dribbled out, and I could see a leaf or two falling real soft from the birch tree there at the side. The leaves were narrow and curled, and they looked nice in the sun. But it didn't matter. The clock was ticking and the Thunder was down and in about two seconds, Jasper Jasmine was going to light some simple fool up one more time.

VI

Rooster

I WAS DOWN IN THE BASEMENT, watching the Thunder play the Pacers, and the game was very much of a problem. Jasper Jasmine had just dished the ball to his big galunky center, Rooster Oosterbaan, who's from somewhere like Denmark or Argentina, and Rooster took a step and then collapsed like he ran into a cement wall.

The trainer came out and then the doctor and other guys, and they helped Rooster off the court. The announcer said it looks like the big Dutchman has a blown-out knee.

That's not what Jasmine needs. Even though Rooster Oosterbaan is kind of spazzy, he's a really big guy and he fills up a lot of room for the Thunder. If the Thunder is going to win the NBA championship, they need all their guys, and everybody knows you've got to have a big guy in the middle. It's like Mr. Raltney says, you can teach a lot of things but you can't teach tall.

While I was thinking about this, I heard them start arguing again. It was slow at first, but then it picked up until it sounded like a couple of dogs howling at each other. Lulu and Mom could fight over a piece of dirt. Lulu slammed a door, it sounded like. What else was new. Then I could hear footsteps on the floor upstairs, and then I heard the door open to the basement and stomping shoes coming my way. *Uh-oh.* I sat up instead of lying on the couch, and I tried to turn the TV off, but I was too late.

"Is that stupid TV on again?" said Mom. "Are you going to waste your life watching basketball? I don't know how much more of you kids I can take. You don't clean your room, you don't have a job, you don't provide anything around here but laziness. You are so selfish. All you think about is yourself."

She was pretty wound up. I didn't want her to be mad at me, but I didn't know what to say when she was like this. *How could I get a job,* I was thinking. *I'm only eleven.* But maybe I should have one anyway, doing stuff like mowing somebody's grass instead of just our own.

She saw my inflatable beach ball that is like a basketball, and she picked it up and pulled the plug and started squeezing the air out of it.

"This is what my life is like," she said, squeezing.

She looked at me with her teeth together and her mouth open. I didn't know what she was talking about.

"Just like this," she said. "Just like this."

She was screaming it. Then she was just saying it and squeezing. It made me real uncomfortable, and I sat there and felt awful. She squeezed until the ball was just a wrinkled piece of plastic. Then she threw it down and started sobbing and went up the stairs.

Rooster

I turned off the TV because I didn't want her to be mad. Then I sat on the couch and was quiet. Then I got up and took my Thunder schedule from the place where I keep it behind the TV. I sat down again. I had a lot of things on my mind. But I looked at the schedule and thought about who the Thunder were playing and who they would have a hard time with and who they would slaughter and how much they would miss Rooster. Then I thought about Jasper Jasmine and his long arms and his smile, and I wondered if he ever had any problems in his life.

VII

Hide-and-Seek

IT WAS SATURDAY AGAIN, and I was trying to forget about school. Some of the guys were playing pickup ball at the rec center, but I didn't go because Mom was still angry about basketball and I thought I'd try to keep her calm for awhile.

The sun was out, and a couple kids came by. They weren't looking for me, but they stopped near our side yard because we have a patch of blackberry bushes near the gully, and a lot of times kids will stop and pick berries at this time of year and eat a bunch or put them in a pot or a cup or maybe a paper sack. I walked over after a while just to see if they wanted to play.

"Hey, Dimmy," said Charlie Bratcher. He's in the fourth grade and he lives down at the end of the road. He was with a little kid that probably was a cousin or somebody like that who he had to babysit.

"Hi, Charlie," I said.

I sat down in the grass, and after awhile, Charlie and the little kid sat down, too. They ate some blackberries, and their fingers started turning purple. That's another thing that is funny about life: Why are blackberries purple? Why aren't groundhogs hogs? How can it rain cats and dogs?

"Want one?" Charlie asked, holding up the last of his berries.

"No, but thanks," I said.

"Hey, Charlie," I said. "Does your buddy have a name?"

"Yeah, he's Jeff. He's eight."

"Does he talk?"

"When he wants."

"Does he ever play games or stuff?"

"Sure, I think so."

We sat for a while, and then I lay down. The sky was a color of blue that almost hurts it's so pretty. There were clouds that looked like sheep above the McMahons' house.

"Charlie, do you see a toad with a toothpick in his mouth?" I asked.

"Nope," he said.

All three of us were lying down now, because they were done with their blackberries.

"I see a milk truck getting ready to crash," he said. "Do you?"

"Where?"

"Over there."

"No. I see a baby kitten or something. A bear."

We lay there and just looked up.

After a while two more kids rode their bikes down the sidewalk and stopped. Eddie and his sister, Edith. Eddie was I think in third grade, and Edith was pretty large and, like, in seventh grade. She was good at art, because I saw her paintings on the wall at school and they looked like somebody who was a teenager had made them. They stood with their bikes between their legs and one foot on a pedal.

"Guys," I said, "you want to play hide-and-seek?"

"What kind?" asked Eddie.

"Like in the yard and the woods. You can't go forever, but you can hide in good places. No indoors."

"What's home base?" Charlie asked. Then he answered himself and said, "That big weeping willow tree. You have to touch it. No kings. No freebies. No time-outs."

"With both hands," said Eddie.

"No safeties or fast counting."

We all were standing now, and it seemed like a good idea to play hide-and-seek, it being such a great day.

Then the little kid, Jeff, finally said something.

"Who's it?" he asked.

"Last one to the tree," said Edith, who was about halfway there already.

Nobody moved for a second, then we went flying off to touch the tree, and naturally the little kid, Jeff, got there last and he said he wasn't playing and he was going home, and he started to cry. So Charlie said, "Hey, come back; you're not going anywhere. Take it easy. I'll be it." And so Charlie was.

He was mad about it, but that's what happens when you have to take care of a little kid who's kind of a brat.

Charlie stayed by the weeping willow tree while the rest of us backed up. "Okay, I'll count to twenty-five by a thousand-and-ones," he said. "No cars or anything like that. You gotta be by yourself, and all I gotta do is see you and then beat you back here, and ties go to it, and no tripping. And, Jeff, if I get you, you're it or you can go back and put a diaper on."

Charlie put his head on the tree and closed his eyes. "A thousand one, a thousand two . . ."

We bolted. Edith went one way and Eddie went the other and Jeff just ran like a nutcase to the other side of the yard and then ran across the street and hid behind the garbage cans in the Peronis' driveway. Me, I took off into our backyard and then down the hill into the woods.

Down the steep side I went, running and feeling good and excited like an animal. The sun came through the leaves in speckles of light and heat, and it felt soft on my skin and sometimes almost blinded me for a second. I went through the swampy parts and then I curved up the bank a little bit, and there was a big maple tree that had branches just about at my head. I looked at it and up the trunk. *Perfect.* I jumped and grabbed a branch and swung my leg over and pulled myself up. Then I started to climb.

When I got up about as high as I wanted to go, there was a very fat branch that was almost flat on its top. I shinnied out a ways and then with my feet propped up on two branches that came out from that big branch, I lay down. I put my hands behind my head, and I was pretty sure nobody was going to find me. You'd almost have to be a squirrel to find me is what I was thinking.

So I lay there and thought about a lot of things. I tried to think about myself as an adult, but I couldn't do it. How could I wear a suit and say stuff like: Why don't we have lunch? How could I ever be in a war? Could you be a kid your whole life? I wondered. If you just didn't grow up? How did your brain go from being this kid that liked basketball and cartoons to liking stuff like newspapers and martinis? Didn't you have any control over things like that? If kids could see what they were going to be when they were older, they'd probably take a lot of precautions to avoid it. But you grew, and I guess you couldn't stop no matter what.

Then I heard something. It was all the kids walking through the trees and brush real slow and jabbering away.

"Are you sure he came down here?" Charlie asked.

"Yeah, he went this way," said Eddie. "He went into the woods and then he disappeared."

"Well, we better find him or this is really stupid," said Edith.

The kid, Jeff, was way on the edge, and he was kicking logs and poking things with a stick.

"Maybe he has a secret hiding place," Jeff said.

Then, oh my god! I realized they would never see me up here and they would keep on walking and looking and if they went far enough, they would find my fort. I freaked. What was I going to do? I sat up, and there was a vine coming down the maple tree and it looked fresh and strong. I crawled over to it and tugged on it. It seemed sturdy. I grabbed hold and started to go down it as fast as I could. I was up higher than I thought, and when I got to about where the first floor on a house is I could feel the vine starting to rip and slide down the tree.

"Yow!" I yelled, and then the vine pulled away completely, and I crashed through a small branch and fell all the way to the ground.

I landed on my back in some leaves and dirt with a *woomp*, and Charlie yelled, "I see him! Run, run, everybody!"

They all went flying back up the hill through the trees, screaming like maniacs. I got up and took some deep breaths. I was dizzy and my neck hurt. Pretty quick, though, I felt a lot better. That was no way to come down a tree, believe me. I was okay, but I was lucky, too.

When I got back to the weeping willow tree, they were all there sitting around.

"You're it," said Eddie.

"Yeah, I know," I said. But I wasn't really thinking about that.

I was thinking about how close I'd come to disaster. Which would be my fort getting discovered and all my secrets being gone.

VIII

The Elbow

AT PRACTICE ON THURSDAY, the most amazing thing happened. Chet "Chewy" Looey had gotten sick at lunch and had to call his mom and go home. We had a scrimmage planned for when we were done with drills, and now there were only ten of us and I had to play, and this was one of the best things ever to happen to me.

It wasn't that Coach Raltney wanted me to play. I had to play. You needed five guys on each side, and Larry the manager was so skinny and dorky that you couldn't even think about putting him in. I don't mean he was a dork—he was an okay guy. He was just dorky whenever you put a basketball in his hands. He made me look like Allen Iverson or somebody. Plus, he was scared of playing, and I bet if Coach Raltney had told him he was going to be in the scrimmage, he would have quit on the spot.

The Elbow

So we divided up, and I was on the team with Luke Delgato, Billy McReynolds, C. W. May, and Vance Lester. Naturally, we needed Vance to make up for the addition of me. But that was cool. I was in full agreement with Coach Raltney on that one. One not-so-good guy offset by a star like Vance—that's the way you do it.

"Dimwit, try not to screw things up," Coach Raltney said, looking sort of upset. "Just, just . . ."

Then he walked away.

"I can't believe you're on my team," said Vance, shaking his head. "Stay out of my way, and if you ever get the ball, give it to me, or I'll dunk you in the garbage can."

We were blue, and the scrimmage started with the red team taking the ball out and bringing it up court. We were in a man-to-man, and I was guarding Kenny Koski. I was pretty fired up. I guess I bumped into Kenny a few times, and once I tripped and slammed into him and Luke and then came flying back the other way.

"Man, Rob," said Kenny. "Calm down."

Somebody shot and the ball bounced off the rim. It went right over my head before I could even move. Things were happening really fast. And right away I was breathing hard, and I knew I wasn't playing too smoothly. Coach Raltney would look at me every now and then, and he would just roll his eyes.

"I mean it, Rob. Knock it off."

"What?"

"You're hacking me," said Kenny, "and you're, like, nuts."

The whistle blew.

"This is basketball, not hockey, Dimwit," said Coach Raltney.

So I backed away from Kenny, and before I knew it, he got the ball and made a shot right in front of me.

So now I was confused, and I couldn't help myself; I started playing a little wilder again.

The ball came loose on offense, and it was bouncing toward me. I grabbed it. For just a tiny second, I held it without moving and felt it in my hands, so sweet and full of good things. Somehow it felt better than usual because this was actually a scrimmage, and not just me shooting by myself or racking the balls.

Kenny had tripped going after the ball, and he was still down in a pile with C. W. and Billy, and they were scrambling to get up. Nobody was guarding me, and I wasn't too far from the basket. I didn't see anybody else open, so before I knew it, I was taking a shot. I was looking at the rim so hard that I didn't see Jeremy Broadbill come flying from nowhere and swat the ball so hard that it grazed off Chump Ernst's head and flew all the way into the bleachers. Jeremy is really tall and muscular, and he can jump to the moon.

When he smacked the ball, he said, "Bye-bye."

A couple of guys were laughing.

Vance Lester looked at me and said, "Leather sandwich."

After Larry ran over and got the ball and we started playing again, all I did was play defense and pass whenever I touched the ball. I passed it right to Vance. He'd said to do that, and why not? There's nothing wrong with being a complimentary player, I figured. For instance, Jake Van Beeker was a complimentary player for the Thunder. He was six-seven with a buzz cut, and he kind of ran like a mechanical man, but he knew just how to help out Jasper Jasmine so Jasper could play his game. Jake Van Beeker was from California, and he liked beach volleyball and I guess he was pretty good at it. The papers called him Surfer Dude. But he wouldn't shoot if Jasper was hot, and he just played a real solid, helpful kind of game. He rebounded and boxed out and played tough D. One time I was watching a Thunder game, and Jake Van Beeker had a sure lay-up, but he turned all the way around and threw the ball way out to Jasmine at the three-point line, and Jasper drilled a bomb, and I was a Jake Van Beeker fan from then on.

So I decided to rebound like Jake, too. I missed a couple balls that bounced off the rim, and then I saw one that I could get. I crouched down and tried to jump as high as I could, swinging my arms up and everything. And then the lights went out.

When I woke up, I was lying on the gym floor. I could hear voices but I couldn't see anything or tell what anybody was saying. Then I saw some faces and I heard somebody say, "Man, he got crunched." My nose hurt real bad, and now I could see blood all over the place. I tried to sit up.

"Stay down for a minute," said Coach Raltney. Larry handed him a white towel, and he pushed it under my nose and boy did that hurt. He pulled it away, and it looked like a red sun in the middle.

"Man, I'm sorry," said Jeremy Broadbill. "Bro, you, like, threw your nose into my elbow."

Finally they let me sit up, then stand up. I started to walk to the sideline, and then I almost dropped to the floor again. It was a very unusual feeling, like my knees had no kneecaps in them or something.

"Easy, easy," said Coach Raltney.

Larry, and Luke Delgato, helped me to the bench, and I just sat and held the towel to my nose, and every now and then I took it down and was amazed at how red my blood looked on the white. I was looking at it and looking at it and then I was waking up again.

"Hey, somebody call his mom," said Coach Raltney. "He's going in and out of it. The number's in my office."

The players were standing looking at me lying there on the bench. They were fuzzy, and their voices were like static.

"Is he blablah?" somebody asked.

"Blar neth sum allo."

Bbbbbbnnnnnn . . .

The next time I woke up, I was sitting in my mom's car. She was driving, and the radio was on. I listened to the music for a minute, and then I realized it wasn't music, it was just the engine and my head pounding. Mom wasn't happy. She was yelling at me and telling me how stupid basketball was.

"Here you are with a broken nose and blood all over, and I had to leave my job early because of this dumb game and this dumb boy who thinks he's in the NBA."

The car hit a bump and that didn't feel good to my head.

"You never play, and then this is what happens when you do," she said.

I didn't say anything.

I didn't feel too hot. I couldn't breathe, except through my mouth. And I didn't want to argue. Jeremy had some kind of elbow. He must have had a steel plate in his elbow. *Man.*

"You won't be playing that game anymore, that basketball, I can tell you that, Buster," she said.

She, like, turned to make sure I heard her. I started to say something, but I couldn't even do that. She was making me hurt more. She was making me feel miserable.

"This foolishness will end, and you'll have plenty of duties around the house. I don't ever want to see a basketball again. You hear me?"

She looked at me, and I made a little noise, but I just couldn't argue with her. But something hit me right then as we were driving down the road. I knew how to solve everything. I knew what to do.

I was going to run away.

IX

Leaving Home

I WENT TO SLEEP, and the next day, I didn't go to school. The day just drifted by off and on like a dream that you wake up from and then while you're thinking about what the dream was, you fall asleep again. I ate dinner with Mom and Lulu, but I wasn't very hungry. Mom wasn't freaking out anymore. Mostly she was just silent. Lulu stared at me and kept saying I looked like somebody who should be in a monster movie.

"No, I know what you are," she said. "You're an actor who got a bad nose job."

After dinner I went back to my room and fell asleep thinking about Sol and Flossie. I dreamed Flossie was the size of a cow and had a web made out of climbing rope.

The next morning, I woke up and just lay in bed and felt rotten. My nose had a bump in the middle of it, but it wasn't as full of junk as it was the day before, and it didn't bleed anymore. My head ached but mostly only if I tried to think too hard. Around ten I went into the kitchen and fixed myself a bowl of cereal. I sat there and ate, and then I poured some orange juice and drank that. I turned on the TV because it was Saturday and I figured there would be cartoons or a kids' show on. But I turned the TV off after about five minutes because it bored me and there was the same stupid mouse running all over getting chased by the even stupider cat. I sat in my chair and looked at nothing. All I could hear was the clock *tick-tock*ing. For a while I thought this could go on forever. I just heard the clock, and my mind was blank.

Then somehow I moved. I went into my room and got dressed and picked up a few things off my dresser and put them in my pockets and backpack. I got some stuff from my drawers and some apples from the refrigerator and a half loaf of bread from the breadbox. I went back to my room and stood on a chair in the closet and got my old sleeping bag, the lumpy little thing, from up high, and squashed it into my backpack. I walked out of the house. Mom and Lulu were gone, and the day was very sunny and windy.

I went into the woods and down my path to the fort. I went inside and lit a candle. Everything looked okay. It was quiet inside, and I looked for Solomon and found him in his terrarium. He was cold, but when I held him for a while, he warmed up and started walking on my hands and then up my arm. Flossie was in the corner of her web, doing nothing. She looked just like the Flossie in my dream, except about a million times smaller. My head felt a lot better, especially if I didn't shake it too fast.

I pulled out my Thunder schedule and looked at it.

"Today is the tenth, isn't it?" I asked Solomon.

He didn't say anything, so I looked at one of the army guys.

Indeed it is, sir! he yelled.

"Then tomorrow is the eleventh."

Yes, sir.

I folded up the schedule, and then I put Solomon back in his terrarium. I grabbed some chewing gum from root five and I tidied the rug a little bit. I lined up all the army guys in order on root seven, with the standing ones in the back, then the kneeling ones with rifles, and finally the lying-down ones in the front. "Protect the fort," I said. Then I blew out the candle and opened the flap and went out.

I walked up through the woods to the road and walked past my house, out toward the highway. I found the bike path that goes along beside the highway for a long way, and I started walking down it. The sun was so bright, it hurt my eyes and made my head throb. But after a while the walking felt sort of comfortable, and I got into a rhythm. I pretended I was a soldier marching to someplace he didn't know where he was going.

But I knew where I was going. I was going to the city.

X
The Train

AS I WALKED ALONG, people passed me every now and then. Most of them were on bikes, all hunched over and speeding by. But one guy who passed me was an old man who was sitting up straight on a really ancient-looking bike that had a tall pole coming off the back fender with an animal tail, maybe a fox tail, flapping on top. He nodded when he went by, but he didn't say anything. Then three girls on Rollerblades went by, with one of them skating backwards. All three were yakking like crazy. Then it was quiet for a while until a guy running in a shiny sweat suit went flying by me from behind making a *swooshing* sound. He startled me because he came out of nowhere, but then two seconds later, his big brown dog went flying past scaring me all over again.

Nobody else went by for awhile. I spent a lot of time looking at the leaves and flowers and bushes that were along the sides of the path and wondering what they looked like when it was spring or summer. I stopped to look at a monarch butterfly sitting on a milkweed pod that was open and empty. I watched his wings go up and down slowly. I knew he could taste things with his back legs, but he probably wasn't eating anymore.

"You need to get flying south," I said. "Go to Mexico, butterfly."

There were houses and a couple parks. There was one place where somebody had drawn a bunch of faces on the path with colored chalk. I looked up just in time to see a guy in a wheelchair come racing toward me. The guy had gloves on his hands and a baseball cap turned around backwards on his head, and when he went sailing by, he said, "All right, brother."

The bike path ended not far after that. There were tall houses all around and streets that were a lot more crowded with cars than where I lived. I knew the train went somewhere along near here and that it went into the city. I walked down the nearest sidewalk, thinking about the train, and then all of a sudden I heard a horn blowing in the distance one, two, three, four times. Then I heard the train itself come *clickety-clack*ing along somewhere behind me, and I realized it was just a couple blocks away. I ran toward it, but by the time I got to the tracks, it had already gone past and was *clacket*ing away.

Well, that was okay, because where would I have gotten on, anyway? I walked along the tracks for about ten minutes until I saw a station around the bend. I went down off the tracks, through the brown dead weeds and over a wire fence, and then I walked along the sidewalk next to the street and entered the station the way you're supposed to. The sign

hanging from the roof above the waiting area said
WOODSIDE. A train came, going the other direction. Then
another one came, just like the first. Finally, a train going my
direction pulled up. The wheels screeched a little, and steam
shot from under some of the cars like big sneezes, and then
the doors opened up. People got off, and the conductors
stepped out from a couple of the cars and looked around. I
waited while an old lady with two shopping bags got on in
front of me, and then I climbed on and took a place by myself
on a green seat that could hold two people.

In a minute a conductor came by and said, "Where to,
sir?"

"Downtown," I said.

"That's five-fifty one way."

I fished around in my backpack and found my wallet. I
took out one of the two ten-dollar bills I had and gave it to
him. He gave me four and a half dollars back, snapping the
bills with his thumb and finger like a magician. He had a
freckled neck and a ponytail that just barely stuck out from
under his blue hat.

"You got people waiting for you down there?" he asked.

I nodded.

"Mom, Dad?"

"Both."

"How old are you?"

"Twelve," I lied.

He reached into his leather purse and snapped out another
dollar and gave it to me.

"Twelve and under is only four-fifty," he said.

The train jerked to a stop, and he walked away. When
the train started again, he came back.

"Reason I ask is sometimes kids go off on adventures and nobody knows it. Sometimes it's not safe. You wouldn't want to be lost."

He looked at me, and I nodded.

"Okay, tiger," he said.

Then he left to take care of the other people with tickets.

Everybody got off at the big station that was the end of the line. I hurried into the crowd so the conductor wouldn't see me and maybe tell somebody that I didn't know what I was doing. There were a million people trying to get through the doors into the station, and inside the station, people were walking in every direction.

I took the escalator down to the ground floor, and when I looked up there was a gigantic clock hanging above me that said it was almost five o'clock. I looked at my nose in the shiny black stones that made up the huge pillars by the front door, and I didn't think it looked too bad. My headache was mostly gone, but now my stomach was growling. Behind me in the station, there were a bunch of food places with doughnuts and hamburgers and tacos and stuff and just looking at those places made my mouth fill with slobber. I went over to the taco place and looked at the menu above the counter. I went to an empty table and counted my money. I had seventeen dollars in bills. And a bunch of change. I had pennies and nickels pretty much filling the bottom of my backpack. I sat down at the table, dumped everything out and started counting the coins.

"Robbed the piggy bank, huh, son," said a man.

I looked up. He was a weird-looking guy with thick glasses on and a big coat. I didn't say anything, and he stood there for awhile. Then he smiled and left.

Four dollars and seventy-three cents in change. That's how much I counted. I went to the counter and ordered the two-taco special with a bean tostada and a medium soda. That was three dollars and fifty-eight cents. With all my change and everything, I had eighteen dollars and fifteen cents left.

I ate my food real fast, and then I couldn't help it—I let out a big long humungo belch. I looked around, but there was too much noise in the place for anybody to know where it came from.

I walked out of the train station, and I saw a man putting people into taxis on the crowded street. I went over to him and asked him if he knew where Commerce Street was.

"Four blocks south," he said.

"Can you tell me which way is south?" I asked.

He pointed and then he was whistling for a cab and yelling to somebody else, and it was like I might as well have been a wrapper blowing past. Well, south was that way, the way he pointed, so I started walking.

There were a lot of cars and buses, and it seemed like everybody really liked to blow their horns a lot. I had been in the city a few times with my mom and once or twice on field trips, like to the museum and the aquarium, with all the kids on the school bus. But I never just walked around like I was doing now. And I'd never been in the city alone.

I crossed the street and looked up at the tall buildings. Now, if you worked in one of those places way up there, wouldn't it be like working on a mountain? Except you're just looking across at another mountain peak where people are looking back at you. And there were all those millions of windows, and none of them opened up. It was probably too cold to open a window today, but what about in the summertime or just if you needed a little fresh air or you had a paper airplane you spent a long time building and you just had to see it sail out and fly wherever it could go? Windows that don't open make no sense to me. But then, maybe the people who are up so high are worried about scary things, and windows that don't open make them feel safe.

I crossed a street, and there was a store with somebody working in the front window, putting up Thanksgiving decorations and taking down Halloween decorations. The lady had a cardboard turkey under her arm, and she was trying to untie a large witch that was hanging from the ceiling. The witch was on a broom that was very old-fashioned and would have been impossible to sweep up dirt with. Or at least you could never sweep up something like the flour I spilled in our kitchen one time, and then Mom went kind of nuts.

I realized I hadn't thought about what Mom would feel about me leaving. I didn't want to think about any of that. I was just doing what I was doing right now. Going away. No thinking. Just going.

Farther down I stopped to look in a coffee store on the corner. Somebody came out holding a covered cup real carefully in his hand, and I could smell the warm smell of coffee and coffee cake coming out of the place. I looked in the long window and saw there was a small fire going in a fireplace in the back and people were sitting in big chairs reading the paper or chatting. Other people were standing in line in front and looked like they were in a hurry. Men with briefcases. Ladies in dresses and running shoes.

"Hey, piggy-bank kid, sure looks good, doesn't it?"

"What?" I said.

I looked up and a man was standing next to me. He had on a big coat, and his eyes were real pale blue. I didn't recognize him at first because his thick glasses were off. They were hanging on a silver chain around his neck. But it was the guy from the train station.

"Come on in, I'll buy you some hot chocolate," he said.

I just stared at him. He opened the door.

"Come on," he said. There was somebody behind me now, and other people were trying to get in the door, so I didn't know what to do, so I just walked in.

"What's your name?" said the man. "Over here. Let's get in line."

The coffee smell was everywhere, and people were jostling around, getting in line or picking up bags of coffee to be ground up or checking out coffee mugs that were for sale, and great big pots and coffeemakers and stuff like that. I didn't know what I was doing in here. I was full from my taco meal. I like hot chocolate, but I didn't need any now, and I just seemed to be stuck here because I couldn't think of anything to say.

The man reached out and pulled me a little into the line so other people could get past, and he kind of held onto my coat.

"I'm Mr. Williams," he said. "A good old-fashioned coffee drinker and a guy who's always looking for talented kids. You're probably wondering what I do. I'm a talent scout, that's my business. Do you have any talents?"

Before I could say anything, the lady asked what we wanted to drink.

"Coffee for me and hot chocolate for my nephew," said the man.

I looked through all the people, and I could see that the coffee shop went in an L shape with an entrance on two streets. When the lady was putting the drinks on the counter, I said to the man, "I have to use the bathroom over there. I'll be right back."

He blinked real fast, and his eyes scared me because they were so cold and the pupils were little, and he said, "Okay, hurry right back over here."

I nodded, and then I wormed through the crowd, around the corner, and past the place where people were putting sugar and milk in their coffee. Then right before the restrooms, there was the other exit door. I ducked down and looked through the crowd back at the man and he was looking my way like he had lasers for eyes, but he couldn't see me because I was down so low. The door was there, and—*zip*—I darted through it while somebody was coming in, and I just started running like a crazy boy.

I ran straight and fast for blocks and then I saw the Commerce Street sign, and I turned right, and my shoes barely touched the ground. I could see the street signs as I flew past one corner after the other. It was cold, and I was breathing hard, but it didn't matter. I felt like I could run forever, and I would to get away from that guy. Slowly the big buildings started to turn into smaller buildings and then into places that looked like regular businesses and some small apartment buildings. I stopped sometimes to look behind me, but there was nobody there. There were vacant lots after a while and junked-up old cars parked in the street, with a lot of trash lying around. I slowed down and trotted, and then I slowed down even more and walked. I was panting, and my heart was beating hard.

There was a liquor store across the street, and out front some men were drinking out of paper bags and waving their arms while they talked to each other. They looked at me for a second, but then they looked back at each other and went on talking and waving. I walked past a parking lot in front of a building that was surrounded by a high chain fence with barbed wire on top. A nasty-looking dog skidded up to the fence from the inside, and I jumped back into the gutter. He was howling and drooling and barking like crazy. I thought I was dead, for a second, but he couldn't get to me. He bashed into the fence, but it wasn't going to break. His fur was standing up like a dinosaur's ridge down the middle of his back. He was mad, but he was still just a dog.

"Sit!" I yelled.

He kept barking.

"Sit!" I yelled again.

Then I said it softer. "Sit. Just sit."

I bent down and held my finger by my face, and I shook it at him one time and said, "Sit."

I couldn't believe it. He sat down.

He couldn't get near me because of the fence, but I didn't care. I didn't want him acting like a nutcase just because he was a dog and I was a boy. That made no sense. "Nice doggy," I said. He was wagging his tail and whining and looking at me real hard.

"Stay," I said.

He tilted his head.

"Stay."

Then I slowly backed away and walked down the sidewalk. When I got to the end of the fence I said,

"Okay," and man he came flying toward the fence again and crashed into it and started barking like a maniac again.

I left him behind and walked up the street until there was nothing but parking areas and gravel lots. I was tired all of a sudden—I mean really tired—and I needed someplace to lie down. Someplace safe. I could tell this wasn't such a great part of town. My nose hurt, and my head ached a little. There were a couple trees together, but they were right by the street and weren't much protection. There was a huge construction hole dug in one of the lots and piled up near the hole were a bunch of round cement things. Some of them were gigantic and must have weighed tons. They were like pipes that you could fit together if you were a giant and wanted to make a cement tube for water maybe, or even a small river. I walked into one, and I didn't even have to bend. There were other pieces that got smaller and smaller, and I kept walking in and out of them until I came to this one section that was about ten feet long and maybe three feet high. There were weeds near one end, and at the other end there were a bunch of pieces of other pipes that lay real close and fanned out like fingers.

I climbed through the weeds into the pipe and looked around. A streetlight trickled lines of soft light on the bottom. The pipes at the other end protected that side, and if I had to run, I could zip down that way and take off through any of the sections that fanned out, and that would confuse somebody who was chasing me, because they'd have to guess which pipe I was in. Naturally, the floor of the pipe was curved, and that was strange. But I put my backpack on it and pulled out my old Cub Scout sleeping bag and put it down on the curved cement. The bag was pretty short, because I have grown since I was eight, which was when I got it. But I lay down, and I don't know why, but I was exhausted and it was all I could do to untie my shoes and put them beside me without breaking my jaw from yawning. I lay there and listened to the night sounds, and I heard a siren way far off and cars driving down other streets and then a big truck grinding up Commerce Street. I saw a rocket ship land real soft in the field nearby and hundreds of turtles climb off, and that's when I realized I was asleep.

XI

The Thunder Dome

I WOKE UP TO THE SOUND of somebody yelling, "Red Top! Come on in!" the voice hollered. "Parking all day, easy out! Red Top! Bring 'er in! Hey, parking!"

I crawled to the end of the pipe and looked through the bushes. Cars were parking all over the place. I knew why. I put on my shoes and rubbed my eyes and put my sleeping bag back in my knapsack. I ate my apples and had three pieces of bread. There were two sort of squashed pieces left, and I put them in my pocket. I hid my backpack behind some rocks just outside the pipe. Then I climbed out of the pipe and trotted over to the sidewalk and started walking like a normal person. I looked across the street.

There it was. The Thunder Dome. Home of Jasper Jasmine. Home of the greatest player in the history of the planet.

I looked at my watch. Boy, I slept late. It was almost eleven o'clock. The game started at noon. Thunder against the Lakers. What a game. A *big* one.

As I walked, the crowds of people got bigger. There were groups of men and whole families and even guys with fancy women who looked like they were going to church or a PTA meeting or something. It was Sunday, so maybe they *were* going to church, but I doubt it. There were cops around, directing traffic, and buses and taxis everywhere.

I went up to the building and then toward a sign that said GATE 6. Near the big glass doors there were a lot of little kids playing on the statue of Jasper Jasmine that was so amazing I thought I was going to pass out. The statue was huge and it was sort of in the private parking lot and it had a low iron fence around it. Jasper had a ball in one hand, and he was sailing backwards toward a metal hoop that was part of the statue, and he had this smile on his face that let you know he was going to ram that ball through there and give somebody a serious, serious facial.

The statue was huge, and mothers kept yelling at their kids to stay off it and don't climb over the fence, but nobody paid any attention to their moms. Kids climbed right onto Jasper's shoulders. "Be careful or you'll fall off and break your head open like an egg," yelled one mom. But the kids swarmed the thing, and lots of people took pictures with their cameras.

I looked around, and then I hopped the little fence and went right up to Jasper and climbed past two boys in Thunder jackets. I palmed the metal ball with Jasper. *Yeehaw.* We prepared to do the monster-dunk thing, me and my man, Mr. Jasmine.

I got down after a while and I went up to a line of people waiting to buy tickets. When I got to the window, a man behind the glass spoke through a microphone. "What's the name?" he said.

"Denwood," I said. "Robby Denwood."

He looked through a stack of envelopes, and then he said, "I don't see it. You sure you got will-call?"

"What's will-call?" I asked. "I just need a ticket for me. The best you got."

"This is a sellout," said the man. "And you're in the will-call line."

"Oh, sorry." I just stood there.

"A sellout," he said again. "All that's left are a few standing-room only. Top of the three-hundred level. Go over to that line and maybe you can get one. Next."

I walked over to another line, and after a while I got to the window and I said to the lady, "One, please."

"Nothing but standing room," she said.

"That's okay. I'll take one," I said.

"Twenty-five dollars," she said.

"What! Really? Don't you have a cheap one for eighteen dollars?"

"They're all the same. Twenty-five. That's it."

I opened my wallet. "All I got is eighteen dollars and fifteen cents."

"Sorry. The price is printed. No discounts."

I walked away. Oh no. What could I do?

I walked around on the sidewalk outside the building, slowly, just going in circles. Every now and then a door would stay open for a while, and I could hear the sound of the crowd and the music inside.

I saw a guy in a green winter coat walking and saying real soft, "I got tickets. Hey, I got tickets."

I went up to him and said, "Can I buy one? I got eighteen dollars."

"No. Beat it," said the guy. "I'm getting a hundred minimum."

I didn't go away. I walked right beside him.

"Please. I came a long way and I have to get in. I'll take your worst ticket, anything, and I'll give you everything I have, eighteen dollars and fifteen cents."

The man stopped. "All right," he said. "Gimme your money. Here's a ticket, a lousy one. And you gotta go in through gate twenty-two, on the other side."

I gave him my money, even the coins, and took the ticket and said, "Thanks." Then I ran for the other side of the huge stadium. But there wasn't a gate twenty-two. The gates stopped at twenty. So I went to gate twenty and gave the man my ticket. He looked at it and then he handed it back.

"This is a ticket for last Wednesday's game," he said. "You need today's. Sunday."

Oh no, oh no. I ran back around to the other side of the building, but the man who sold me the ticket was gone. Did he know the ticket was no good? Maybe he just made a mistake. Maybe. Yeah, right.

But now the sidewalks were getting empty.

A noisy group of people came walking toward one of the gates, all of them laughing and talking real loud. They looked like businessmen who were always in a hurry. I walked toward them and stood close to the last man in the group. They went through the metal detectors, and I went through after them. They went to the ticket taker, and as they were going through the turnstile one by one, I wormed my way in front and went through real fast.

"Excuse me, is he with you?" said the ticket taker to the men.

I was walking fast, and I could just barely hear somebody say, "No," and then the ticket taker yelling, "Hey, get back here. Guards!" But I got low and I ran in and out through the crowd until I was a long way away, and nobody paid any attention to me.

I went through one of the big arches off the hallway where all the hot-dog stands were and into the arena. Just then the ref threw the ball into the air down on the court, and oh my god, what a beautiful sight. The floor was bright yellow wood all shiny with painted purple lanes and a beautiful purple-and-black thundercloud full of lightning bolts at half-court. The biggest scoreboard in the world hung right over the center circle. And when the Thunder controlled the tip, a roar went up from the crowd that was an amazing deep sound.

I studied the players, and there he was.

There was Jasper Jasmine standing on the wing, catching a pass from L. C. Quitman and holding it in one hand, giving his man head fakes. His skin was brown, and his uniform was white with purple numbers, and his muscles seemed to flex and flex and ripple all the way from his shoulders to his fingers.

"You'll have to find your seat," said a lady in a red jacket.

It shocked me to hear her voice. I was almost, like, in a trance.

I walked to the aisle and started slowly going around the court. I heard the Electric Company dancing girls, which is what they call the Thunder cheerleaders, lead the crowd in the Thunder's special cheer:

The Thunder Dome

Thunder, thunder
Thunder-ation!
We're the Jasmine
Dele-gation!
When we fight with
Determi-nation
We create a
Jasper Nation!

I was up pretty high, so when I saw steps going down a level, I went that way, and before long I was almost at court level. Ushers kept asking for my ticket, and I said it was with my dad at his seat and I think it's right over there. They didn't believe me, but I'd just move on, and as I was walking, I'd get to watch the Thunder and Jasper Jasmine do amazing things for a little longer. Then I'd stop and say, "Oops, it must be over in that section," and do it all over again.

I slowed down for a while, and for a couple of minutes I was standing and not moving at all, because I was just amazed at how hard the players were pushing on each other and how high they were jumping and all this amazing squeaking from their shoes sounding like mice or a bunch of wheels that needed grease.

The Thunder weren't as big as the Lakers, and they got pounded sometimes on the boards. The one huge guy for the Lakers, Battleship Purple, seemed to just knock anybody away whenever he wanted, and when he went in for a jam, he did his Battleship Bellow, and you could hear him roaring louder than the horn. The Thunder missed old elephant Rooster just because he took up a lot of room underneath and could sort of block guys like Battleship out. But Jasper

Jasmine got some big rebounds by soaring over the top of Battleship and the Lakers' other star, Prometheus Lee. And man, did he kill the Lakers on offense when he had the ball and he would make those moves like he was an acrobat going to the hoop. Sometimes he almost seemed to fly. He would rise up into the air and then be moving real slow like someone with a parachute.

The game was tied at 95 with three minutes to go, but Jasper Jasmine kept getting fouled and he made six out of seven free throws down the stretch, and the Thunder won 105 to 101. Jasper Jasmine had forty-one points. The crowd gave out a huge cheer, and Jasper Jasmine saluted everyone and bowed his head, and then he trotted off the court. Eduardo Jackson, who is the Thunder's crazy player with a million tattoos and a pretty bad attitude and all kinds of earrings but a great vertical, climbed on the scorers' table and pulled off his jersey. He waved it around his head a few times like a helicopter while the crowd went nuts, and then he threw it to some lady with blonde hair and a dress that wasn't really big enough for her.

I pushed through the crowd, and before I knew it, I had gotten past the ropes and the chairs and I was walking in the middle of the trainers and managers and people and I just floated along with them right under the stands, past a couple cops and a bunch of ushers and guards into this big bright hallway that led to the locker rooms. I walked like I knew what I was doing, but mostly I stayed little and didn't draw any attention to me.

There were TV camera crews all over the place. There was, like, one guy in fancy clothes with all kinds of makeup on, and behind him there were two regular guys huffing and puffing, one of them with a real heavy camera and the other with a microphone on a long pole, and they all walked along like they were hooked together by ropes. There were lady reporters, and there were foreign people from everywhere talking in different languages. There were a whole bunch of Japanese TV people and writers and guys with tape recorders, and they were running around bowing to each other and anybody they bumped into. I saw a couple actors I recognized from a movie I saw last year, and there was a real pretty lady who was in this TV commercial for beer and who I think was waiting for Eduardo Jackson because I saw them together in this magazine ad for perfume or something. I stood at the back of the crowd in a room with a lot of lights, and I watched Ben G. Bancroft, the Thunder coach, walk up to the front, with two guards by him, and answer questions and talk to reporters about how the Thunder had won the game. He said, "You fellows are aware I taught Jasper Jasmine everything he knows," and then he winked, and all the reporters and TV guys laughed hysterically, even the foreign ones.

When Ben G. Bancroft was done, the guards led him away, and then everybody just turned around and started swarming the other direction out the door and down the hall. I almost got trampled, so I went along with the crowd and kind of got sucked right around the corner and into a smaller room where players were crunched up in front of their lockers. There was a chalkboard pushed to one side and a huge glass refrigerator filled with water bottles and sports drinks, and the video screens hanging up near the ceiling were rerunning the game. Some writers went to a couple of the Thunder lockers on the left, but almost everybody else piled right up to one locker that I couldn't even see, but I knew who it must belong to. There was a lot of shouting and shoving, and this one microphone guy almost slugged another microphone guy, and the language, which was mostly English, was pretty bad.

I took a couple steps closer and jumped up to see what I could. Then I heard a yelp, and I looked up and down. I was standing on Eduardo Jackson's toe.

"Yo, man," he said, "mind if I keep that toe for the Pistons?"

"Oh, sorry," I said.

I backed away, and I couldn't believe all the tattoos on him. He had on his pants and socks but no shoes, and he had a towel over his shoulder. I was looking right at a crocodile that was crawling underneath some dice, which were under a bunch of flowers on Eduardo Jackson's chest.

He put on sunglasses and looked at me. He shook his head, which was dyed orange—at least his hair was.

"Dang," he said. "Sportswriters start early don't they?"

Then he left, and I watched him push his way past everybody, saying, "Nope, nope, nope," every time a writer or camera guy tried to get him to answer a question.

It got quiet all of a sudden, with lots of shuffling feet and pushing, so I got down low again and started wiggling and sliding my way through everybody until one guy elbowed me and I tripped and fell, and when I got up and bumped my way into the clear, I was squashed in with everybody else but I was standing right in front of Jasper Jasmine.

He was talking in a very calm, low voice, and there must have been two thousand microphones in his face. He was tall and he had on this beautiful suit and a blue tie that looked different shades of blue depending on how the light bounced off it.

This is what he was saying: "I try to maintain my composure on the floor. There are moments in every game when the tension rises and you may feel your muscles tightening and the noise level distracts you. That's when you have to relax. Coach Ben calls it the ability to quiet the mind. And that's what it is."

Then everybody jabbered different questions to Jasper Jasmine all at once. I couldn't make out any of them. All I could do was think, My god, here I am. I am here. Jasper Jasmine. Oh my god. I couldn't help myself. I reached out just a little bit and touched the edge of his coat and felt it all smooth. I rubbed it between my thumb and pointer finger.

I don't know what happened—maybe I was saying his name out loud and I didn't even know it—but all at once I looked up and Jasper Jasmine was looking down at me. I let go of his coat. It was almost silent.

"Hi," he said.

"Hi," I said.

"Like the fabric?"

I didn't know what to say, so I just laughed real nervously.

"I'll bet you're from the *Post*," he said. "Getting that new angle. This would be the short one."

Everybody laughed.

Jasper Jasmine kept looking at me, and I think my face was really red. But he patted my shoulder, and I looked up. For some reason, I just said, "Mr. Jasmine, do you ever feel like you're flying?"

The next second there was a guard beside me, and he grabbed my arm and squeezed it, and said in a whisper, "Would you step over here for a moment, son?" He pulled me out of the crowd real fast, all the way through the locker room and into the hall. He wouldn't let go of my arm, and he didn't seem very nice. Another guard joined him.

"Who are you, kid?" the first guard asked. "What are you doing here?"

"I'm with my dad," I said.

"Where is he?"

I looked around.

"Who is he? What's his name?"

"Thomas," I said.

"Thomas what?"

"Thomas."

"Thomas Thomas?"

The guy was looking at me right in the face. The other guard was just standing there.

"Perfect," he said. "Where's your press pass? Where's your ticket? Some ID?"

I fumbled in my pocket with my one free hand. I searched everywhere like I might find it.

"I don't know," I said. "It must have fallen off in all the excitement."

The guy gripped my arm real tight again and started walking fast, dragging me with him. He yelled at the other guard, "Back in a second."

He went down the hall, straight up the stairs into the foyer, and pushed me right out the glass doors onto the side-walk, where there were still a lot of people heading home.

"I'll tell Mr. Thomas you're waiting at gate three," he said. Then he slammed the door and disappeared.

Jerk.

Oh well.

I thought about it for a second. That was me standing talking to Jasper Jasmine. *Whoa.* What a game that was.

Everything so bright and fast, and Jasper doing his thing. I mean, I could almost feel what it was like to be a star. I could feel what it was like to be somebody. I *was* somebody. I was like, I don't know.

No, I was nothing. As usual.

"Yo, yo, buy a paper, small man," a guy yelled at me. He had a bunch of newspapers under his arm. I turned away. It was still daylight, late afternoon. Now what could I do?

I walked down the street and across the parking lot and through the weeds to where my stuff was hidden. I looked inside my backpack. What was there? My sleeping bag. A pair of socks. Nothing. I didn't even have the squashed bread anymore. I guess that was something that *did* fall out in all the excitement.

Now it was time for me to figure out what to do. I hadn't thought this far ahead. Everything had changed since I got smacked by Jeremy Broadbill's elbow. Could I just start walking and walking? Could I walk around in a giant circle, sleep in big cement pipes when I found them, and eat whatever happened to come along? I didn't have any money at all, not even a dime, not even a penny. That was okay, because the game was worth whatever I had, even if I had to sneak in. But there wasn't a lot I could do without money. If I could just do something until the next Thunder game, I'd be okay. I couldn't go home. I wished I could be like a bug, like a fish, like a salamander and hibernate for days and have nothing in my brain—no thoughts, no worries, no nothing—and then wake up and see that golden yellow floor again and hear the squeak of the shoes and the roar of the crowd and watch Jasper Jasmine rule the earth.

I walked a few feet up the sidewalk, but I didn't know why I should keep walking or why I should stop or why I should do anything. I sat down on the curb and looked at the street. It was dusty from all the construction in the area and the cars driving out of the gravel parking lots. But there wasn't any traffic now.

I saw a bug in the gutter, a tiny little guy right below me. What was he doing? How did he know where to go?

"Hello, bug," I said. "Hello, buggie."

I sat and watched him going nowhere. He climbed on top of a pebble and then he climbed down and then he climbed up again. I thought about being eleven. You could climb up and down forever. *Okay*, I said to myself. *Okay, don't do that.* My eyes were sort of filling up again and I was being a baby. *Okay, stop that.* But I couldn't. I thought about Mom for a second, and Lulu and Dad and everything, and I felt so bad. Just useless.

I was crying and I couldn't do a thing about it. A couple little drops of water fell in the dust. *Poof.* They got swallowed up. One ran out to the tip of my nose and I was going to wipe it off, but I didn't because what difference would it make. *Poof.* It landed in the dust.

XII

The Car

"YOU OKAY THERE, HOSS?"

The voice scared me. My brain was far away. I looked up, and there was a car in front of me, a glimmery black one, but the sun was shining from the other side and I couldn't see who was talking.

I scooted back, ready to run. Was it that coffee guy? It didn't sound like him, but I couldn't tell. I wiped my stupid face with my hand and grabbed my backpack.

"Hey, you're that little kid," said the voice.

And now I recognized it. I moved my head and blocked the sun. Oh my god, it was Jasper Jasmine!

"What are you doing out here, watching the dust pile up?"

I shook my head and looked down again. I wasn't that far away from watching my tears fall in the dirt and I wasn't sure if I could talk without blubbering. I was so embarrassed.

But this was amazing. I looked up at the car again, all squinty-eyed in the sun.

"What's up, my man? You lost? I saw you in the locker room, and you don't look like any news reporter I've ever seen."

I could see his face now, with fancy sunglasses on and that beautiful blue suit.

He was smiling.

"Hey, we won the game. No need to be crying."

"I'm not," I said. I looked down again.

"Right," he said. His car chugged with this deep sound like a family of animals inside their den.

I could hear his phone ring. He answered it and told somebody yes, no, he'd sign it tomorrow, Europe was out, fried chicken later, white meat only, he had some business to tend to, bye.

He turned back to me. "You shouldn't just be sitting out here, you know that?" he said. "Why aren't you home? You got a ride? Want me to call somebody? What's up with you, little dude?"

I didn't say anything. For some reason, I felt lonelier than I ever had.

I heard his door open. I peeked up. He climbed out of his car and brushed his pants for a second, and then he sat down next to me on the curb. "Let's just sit and think about this a minute," he said.

He put his head in his hands, just like me. I snuck a look at him. He was looking straight down, studying the dirt. Jasper Jasmine, forty-one points, All-Planet, was messing with me.

The Car

I couldn't help it. I laughed out loud. I laughed so loud and then I was crying and laughing, all at the same time, and Jasper Jasmine was looking at me, chuckling and shaking his head. Another car went by. It slowed down and the driver stuck his head out and gawked and nearly drove off the road.

"All right, get up," said Jasper Jasmine. "I'm taking you home. You're calling Mom, Pop, whoever. But you're getting out of here before it gets nuts. This isn't a real good neighborhood. Plus, this isn't good for my pants."

He stood up and brushed himself off, mumbling.

"The pleats," he said.

He got in the driver's seat.

I stood there. He looked at me kind of annoyed.

"Where do you live?" he said. "Is somebody picking your sad butt up or not? Because I got places to be."

"No."

"No what?"

"Nobody's picking me up."

Jasper Jasmine shook his head. He whistled. He looked at me and blew out his breath.

"Get in," he said. "Just get in."

I wouldn't get in a car with a stranger. But this was Jasper Jasmine, the most famous man on earth. Plus, I was in trouble. Big trouble.

I walked around the front of the car, past this small logo of a gold-and-red horse' on the hood and climbed into the softest leather seat I'd ever been in.

Jasper Jasmine threw my backpack into the little area behind the front seats. There weren't any back seats.

"Is this, like, a race car?" I asked.

"Yeah, and I'm A. J. Foyt. Here." He dropped the phone in my lap. "It's a Ferrari. Call home and tell them—tell somebody—you're on your way."

I looked at the phone. It was tiny and like out of a spy movie.

The car roared and suddenly we were moving. Not real real fast. But in half a second we were going forty. From nothing to forty in a hiccup.

"Call," said Jasper Jasmine.

I looked at the phone but didn't do anything. He looked at me, and we stopped at a light.

"You live somewhere, right? What's your name? You on the lam from the law? What is your deal?"

"No," I said.

"No what?"

"No, I got a home."

"Well, call that home and tell whoever answers the phone you're getting a ride there. Now."

I frowned. I didn't know what to say. I didn't want to call. I didn't want to hear Mom's voice, the answering machine, nothing.

"Okay, okay," said Jasper Jasmine, nodding. "I got it. You ran away from home. Ran away to watch the big basketball team, told Mom and Dad you were never coming back. Ready to make it on your own. Right?"

"My dad isn't here. He's in Texas."

"Well, I'm sorry about that. My daddy died long ago, and I'd rather have him be in Texas, but I'll bet your mom's around, and that's who we're taking you to see. Unless you'd rather I just drop you at the nearest police station."

I looked at him. He had perfect teeth. White like a bath-
tub.

"I guess home," I said.

"And where might that be?"

I told him and he said, "That's a long way off. Gotta be fifty
miles. How did you get here, anyway? Man, you must be serious."

We turned onto the freeway, headed north into the
express lane, and Jasper Jasmine's black car just blasted off
like a missile.

XIII

The Ride

AS WE DROVE ALONG, I told him a lot of things. I told him my name and how old I was and that I had a sister, Lulu, and a mom, and a dad who had driven away one day. I told him that things weren't great at home or at school. I told him how I loved basketball and I thought he was the greatest player in the history of the universe. I told him I hoped Rooster Oosterbaan wasn't through for the year, that even though he had limited mobility, he was a force in the middle. I told him about my school team and jumping for a rebound and Jeremy Broadbill's elbow and about how I remembered lying on the floor of the school gym and then lying on the bench and then lying in a car and then lying in my bed and how it all still made my head hurt to think about it.

"I thought there was something weird about your nose," Jasper Jasmine said. "No offense, but your eyes look like you're wearing mascara."

Then he told me that one time in college he got hit in the side of the head by this player from Southern Cal and that he didn't remember anything about the game at all. Well, he remembered the opening jump ball, and he had fuzzy pictures of the locker room and some guy with a flashlight, but that was all.

"They said I sat on the bench and talked about a lemonade stand I had as a kid, but I don't remember," he said.

He told me his nose had been broken three times.

We were driving fast, but the car didn't bounce at all. It was like an airplane almost, with so many dials and cool things on the dashboard. We were real low to the ground and sometimes almost sailing.

He asked me why I had problems with Mom, and I tried to tell him that she was busy all the time and not real happy and that I was a disappointment to her. I told him that she thought basketball was a waste of time, which it probably was for a guy like me, but not for a guy like him. I tried to tell him that sometimes I felt like I didn't fit in with anything and that I was just so, so . . . nothing special. I tried to tell him that I could feel myself floating away and forgetting about everything when I saw the Thunder play, that I wanted to live inside of a Thunder game, that I wished I could be like the ball, the floor, the lights. I told him I wanted to be the game. I told him I wished I could be him. Just a part of him. Like his shot that went up with that perfect rotation, that perfect arc, that perfect everything, and then it went down so sweet, just so smooth and right and orange, and then the swish, the perfect perfectness. The sound. The flip. The string music. It didn't come out right at all, not the way I wanted to say it, and I turned and looked out the side window because I felt so embarrassed and little and I was going to start *boo-hoo*ing again.

"Buddy," said Jasper Jasmine. "Robby."

I kept looking out the window.

"Hey," he said.

I lowered my head, then I looked over at him with his hands almost making the steering wheel disappear they were so huge.

"Yeah?"

"Listen," he said. We flew past a couple of big trucks. The sun was starting to drop and long shadows criss-crossed the highway. "You're a nice kid. But you can't be me."

We drove a little farther.

"You don't want to be me."

I sort of snorted.

"You think I'm kidding?" he said.

"Yeah."

I looked at him. His face. His suit.

"Who wouldn't want to be you?" I said.

He was quiet for a while. Just the hum of the low, fast car.

"Got a minute?" he said. "Let me tell you a couple things."

XIV

Jasper's Tale

"EVER BEEN TO GEORGIA?"

I shook my head no.

"I'm from Georgia, outside Atlanta. But you probably know that. In the pine woods, but we lived in a housing project. Not a terrible one, but it was a housing project just the same. You knew if you lived there. My dad died when I was six. I have two older sisters and a younger sister and three older brothers. Two of the brothers were so much older, it didn't count, but Eli was close enough that it was a problem. Eli was a good athlete, he could do a lot. But I could play. Do you know what it's like?"

Jasper Jasmine looked at me, and I gave him a wrinkly face. He said, "Well, no, maybe not. But I could just do it." He went on. "There are old videos of me at eight dribbling like a Globetrotter. Eli was good, but not like me; plus he was short. He used to get mad at me for being me. He'd hide my

75

ball, push me around because I made him so mad. But I couldn't stop. I couldn't be what I wasn't.

"Eli set records in grammar school and junior high, and I'd come along two years later and break them all. By the time I was fourteen, there were college recruiters everywhere, and some of them said they were coming around to check out Eli—but he and everybody else knew that wasn't true. I'd even ask some of the recruiters to check him out, let him play with me, let him show his stuff, and sometimes they were almost mean to Eli, saying things as if they didn't care if he heard—about him being too short and whatnot. I didn't like that. But the wall between us just grew.

"And then I got an attitude. I grew more and I used to say to him, 'Okay, you don't like it?' And I'd dunk on him or I'd be mean because I was so fed up, and then I almost enjoyed punishing him on the court. 'Come on, little midget,' I'd say. 'Eat this.' It was cruel, but I couldn't help myself."

He shook his head, and I felt funny because he was telling me this and he seemed kind of sad.

"I know what happened then," I said real fast. "Famous Jackie Stone came to see you, and you loved him and you went to UCLA and played for him and won two NCAAs back to back."

Jasper Jasmine nodded. He looked over at me. "Who'd we beat?"

"North Carolina and Iowa."

"What was my number?"

"Twenty-one as a freshman, then seven for the next two years."

He laughed. "Man, you're something."

"Why were you seven?"

76

We were getting to a part of the highway that was not that far from where my town was. I wanted this ride to last forever.

"I'll tell you why," he said. "Because that was Eli's number in high school and by then I'd lost him. Before my senior year in high school, he left Georgia, went down to Florida, and a couple of years later, got in trouble with the law and ended up in jail. He's out now, and gone somewhere. But back then I felt responsible. I still do. It tore me up. Still does. I wore seven for him. But, Robby, I'd lost a brother and I had basketball to thank for it."

I didn't see exactly what he meant. I think he saw me looking confused.

"Here's the part people don't know. I was ready to sign with Florida State before I signed with UCLA. Know where Florida State is?"

"In Tallahassee?" I said. "That's the capital, isn't it?"

"Right. And Eli was living there, doing whatever he was doing. I did think Jackie Stone was great—man, he had all those banners in the gym at UCLA, all those trophies. But it didn't mean that much to me, UCLA. I knew I was good, and wherever I went, *that* was going to be the place to watch. That was going to be the program. I could have gone to Florida State, and it would have been the same. The Seminoles were *dying* for me to come there. The coach, Samuel Clifton, was cool. I *should've* gone to Florida State. You know why?"

I shook my head.

"Because Eli was in Tallahassee. Right there. If I'd gone to Florida State, I could have looked after him. We could have lived together. We could have been brothers. I could have made them let him into school, maybe even sit on the team bench, scrimmage a little. You know how good that feels, don't you?"

I nodded.

"I know he wanted me to come, even if he never said it. But I didn't. I went as far away as I could. I went to California. Just to show him. What's that? Three thousand miles? Man!"

He shook his head while looking at the road. It was like he had forgotten me and was talking to himself.

"And then Eli was in jail, and then he was out and he disappeared. Everything felt wrong. I hated myself. It was such a simple thing that I could have done. And I blew it. But that little bit changed me. Sometimes I wish I'd never seen a gym floor."

He was quiet for awhile.

"I've told you way more than I should have, partner. But something about you reminds me of me. Is that crazy or what?"

"That's crazy," I said.

"What I'm saying is nobody knows what the inside of a man looks like. Play your own game, Rob. Know what I'm saying? Just use what you have."

I didn't have time to answer, because we were at my exit, I told him, and he swerved the car down the ramp like a racer going fast into a turn. He drove down the road, and before long we were at my house.

"Your mom here?" he asked. He parked his amazing car on our gravel drive.

I went in the house and yelled around, but nobody was there.

"She's not here and neither is Lulu," I said when I came back out. I didn't want him to leave and I wanted my mom to see him. No matter how mad she was going to be. I wanted her to know who I had met and that this was real and I wasn't a complete nothing. Even somebody who hated basketball like her knew who Jasper Jasmine was.

I had an idea.

"Mr. Jasmine, can I show you something?" I asked. "I think you'll think it's cool."

He looked at his watch. He punched some buttons on his phone and read some messages.

"Fast," he said. And he got out of the car.

I took him to the back of our little house and then I smiled.

"Where we headed?" he asked.

"Down there," I said, pointing into the woods. "I'm going to show you way more than I should."

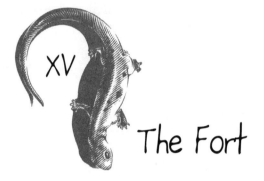

XV

The Fort

THE PATH WAS DRY and bright in the late sun, but it wasn't an obvious path to somebody who didn't know where they were headed. Jasper Jasmine broke off some tree branches as he followed me, I guess so he wouldn't scratch his blue suit. He kept mumbling stuff, but I told him to be careful, please, because this was all totally secret. I stopped a couple times to fix places where he moved leaves out of the way with his fancy shoes.

"You can't be too careful," I said, patting the path.

He snorted and shook his head, and then he pointed ahead. He stopped walking. "What are we doing? You bury bodies down here?"

"We're almost there," I said. "Come on, you'll see."

Then we were in the small clearing and he said, "Okay, enough. I'm not an explorer. It's late. I'm gone."

I walked over to the dead tree, just as he was turning around to leave. I lifted the canvas door that was so camouflaged you couldn't see it, and I said "Ta-da! Mr. Jasmine, sir, I present my fort."

He looked at me and at the hole in the side of the hill and the soldiers and the posters inside, which you could barely see, and he made a face, and he said, "What the hell?"

He came closer and then he moved right up to the cave. "Well, I'll be," he said. "I'll be."

He bent over. Then he said, "You made this thing?"

"Yep," I said.

We both stared inside.

"Well, I didn't dig the hole, but I did everything else."

He frowned. He looked in again. "Dang," he said. "You go in there?"

"Yeah," I said.

He frowned. "I'm going in," he said.

It was tight in the fort, I'll be honest with you. But we both got in there. Jasper Jasmine was pretzeled up at first, but I moved the little stool, and he stretched out more and sort of lay back on root number one.

The candles gave off a nice light, and it was good to see that Flossie was still in her corner and fat as ever. Jasper Jasmine wasn't nuts about Flossie. He told me he and spiders weren't on good terms, but after I explained about her spinnerets and her web-making talents and the fact that if she caught a bug and ate it that was one less bug in the fort, Jasper Jasmine got a little more comfortable about having her around.

Naturally he thought Sol was awesome. I mean, how can you not? He didn't want to hold Sol at first, but when I showed him that Sol wasn't wet but only looked that way because he was so shiny, Jasper Jasmine held him and even let him sit on the sleeve of his coat.

"I had a frog when I was boy," he said. "But this beats a frog sideways."

We shot baskets on my tiny hoop, me sitting up, Jasper Jasmine lying on his back and complaining that this wasn't fair because his hand was too big and the ball was too small and this was my home court and a lot of other stuff. So, when I beat him I said real politely, "Sorry about that," which I'd heard was what he said to Billy Ray Simpson of the Knicks in a playoff game two years ago when he stole the ball from Billy Ray and jammed for the win with three seconds left.

Jasper Jasmine played with a soldier, moving him up to a higher root, and then he chuckled. Then he started shaking his head and laughing.

He looked at me and started to say something, but he shrugged and laughed even harder. Big old belly laughs. And before I knew it, I was laughing, too. It was so funny. All of it. Me and my man, Japser Jasmine. Oh my goodness, we laughed until I thought I'd wet my pants.

XVI

The Jersey

JASPER JASMINE SLAMMED HIS CAR DOOR and looked out his window at me. My mom still wasn't home, and now it was getting dark.

"I have *got* to go," he said. "I haven't had so much fun since payday, little brother, but life calls."

"I just wish my mom could see you," I said. "So she'd know."

I knew nobody was going to believe anything I said about my whole adventure. I didn't even have a ticket stub. Nothing.

"Here," Jasper Jasmine said. He reached under his seat and pulled out something. It was a bag.

"Take it. It's mine," he said.

He handed me the bag, and I opened it. Inside was a Thunder road jersey.

"It was for a charity auction," he said, "but I'll make Fat Abs get me ten more."

I held the jersey, let it unfold all the way down, and stared at it. And then he was gone, just the growl of his car fading away.

Fat Abs. That was Albert Pintcher, the real tall, narrow-shouldered, big-bellied Thunder general manager who nobody liked. Why didn't they like him? Because one time he tried to trade Jasper Jasmine for like six Nuggets and a trillion dollars. The fool.

I held out the jersey with both hands. It was deep purple with a black thunderhead on the chest. On the back it had a black and gold number 7 under the gold name, JASMINE.

I could have worn it as a dress, but I didn't care. I put it on over everything. Let it be a dress. Let Mom see her little boy in a dress. Let everybody see the boy in the dress.

This was some dress. Oh man, this was something!

* * *

Mom got home not long after that.

She showed up with Lulu, and a police car right behind them. They'd been looking all over for me, and mom was out of her mind with worry, she said, and the two cops said I had them scared and that if I hadn't showed up about when I did, they were going to start a manhunt.

I told everybody where I'd been, though I couldn't explain exactly why I left like I did or why I went where I did, because I wasn't sure myself. But I said I didn't want to be a burden to anybody. I meant that. They could see the jersey, and I guess the policemen believed me about being at the game and coming home because they warned me once more and then they left. Lulu said I was a weirdo, like a complete retard. I don't know what Mom thought, but she told me never to do what I did again. Never, ever, ever. She was biting her lip and breathing hard. "Or else, just go away to Texas," she said. "Jasper Jasmine. What's next, Babe Ruth?"

I thought maybe she was going to cry, but she didn't. She looked like a pillow without any stuffing in it. She said I had to come in the house, eat my dinner, and then go immediately to bed. I had to learn. It was not much punishment for what I'd done to her, she said.

"I'm sorry," I said. "I'm sorry."

I really was.

And, naturally, I was grounded. Actually, that was okay. My nose still hurt, and I was pretty worn out. And there was nowhere left for me to go.

XVII

School

ON MONDAY AT SCHOOL, I told Kenny Koski I'd met Jasper Jasmine.

"Yeah, right," he said.

It took me a while to convince him, but when I showed him the jersey and when he saw it was the real thing, he came around pretty much to believing me. But he still didn't understand it.

"You sure it wasn't some guy who looks like Jasper Jasmine?" he said.

"Yes."

"Not a guy in disguise?"

"With a championship ring on and a million-dollar suit and a Ferrari with license plates that say SILK E 7? Don't think so," I said.

"Man, Rob, I don't know how to process this."

"Me, neither. But, Kenny, don't tell anybody. Especially not the team. They'll just laugh at me. Okay?"

"Yeah, sure, Rob."

I went to practice after school, because Mom hadn't said anything specific about no practice. I think it slipped her mind, to tell you the truth. I got dressed and everything, but Mr. Raltney came up to me when I walked out and said, "Uh-uh. You're done for now, mister. You can stand and watch, but you'll need a doctor's letter before I let you on the court."

He squinted and looked at my eyes. He patted my shoulder.

"This could be a good thing, Dimwit. I think God may have been trying to tell you something with that elbow. You ever considered band?"

He went into his office off the gym, and I saw a couple of the guys, including Vance Lester, looking at me and laughing.

Vance came over dribbling the ball and shaking his head.

"Tweet tweet," he said. "Are the lights on?"

I didn't say anything, but I looked under the basket at Kenny Koski who shrugged and mouthed the word *sorry*.

"Did your pal Jasper teach you how to stay conscious on the basketball floor?" Vance said. "Or did you just practice your dunks?"

Luke Delgato came over with Billy McReynolds and Larry Wheeling, the manager. Little Larry was excited. I knew what he was going to say.

"Do you really know Jasper Jasmine?" he asked, all twitchy and big-eyed.

The other guys burst out laughing.

"No," said Vance, "but he's best friends with the tooth fairy."

Everybody went away and I sat on the bench.

Practice was okay, though a little boring. I tried to help Larry with some of his chores, but there really wasn't much to do. I suppose I could have left, but I was waiting to rack the balls at the end because I enjoy that.

But then, after the last whistle, Mr. Raltney saw me going onto the floor just to pick up the balls, and he said, "Uh-uh, you're done. Beat it, big nose."

So that was a lousier ending than I hoped for.

At home I did my homework and then sat in my room and did nothing. After a while I got out the Thunder jersey and put it on my chair. I sat on my bed and looked at it. I kind of lost myself in the purple of it and the threads and the thunderhead.

Somebody knocked on my door, and it startled me, the way a lot of things seem to these days.

"We got a Fed Ex package today," said Mom, "and I don't know why, but it's addressed to you."

I opened the door, and she was standing there holding a cardboard envelope.

"Here," she said handing it to me. "I'd really like to know what's going on around here."

"Why?" I said.

"Who's running this house is what I want to know."

"What, Mom? Who's the letter from?"

She just looked at me.

"Who's it from?"

"The Thunder," she said.

XVIII
The Invitation

THE LETTER WAS ON official Thunder stationery, and it was from Ned Barrowman, Vice President of Marketing and Publicity.

Ned Barrowman said that my presence was requested at the four Thunder games during the next home stand. It was requested that I be the ball boy for those games and that a limousine would be sent for me before each game to expedite transportation and parking problems, and the same limousine would drive me home afterward. One friend could come with me to each game and sit in a mezzanine box with the directors while I worked. I was to please have a parent or guardian sign the enclosed form and mail it back in the attached envelope.

This request had been made by Mr. Jasper Jasmine, a Thunder player, the letter said. Mr. Jasmine hoped and expected I would enjoy this offer. *On to the Championship! Sincerely, Ned Barrowman.*

Oh, yeah. I said to myself. *Oh, yeah.*

Mom had read over my shoulder, and the first thing she said was, "It's a hoax."

"What do you mean?" I said.

"It's fake."

"It can't be," I said. "It's a real letter. It's their real logo."

She shook her head. "Well, you can't go."

"Why not?" I said, almost bawling. Inside, to myself, I said, *Oh please, don't do this to me. Stop being a mother for once. Please.*

"Three of those dates are on school nights, for one thing," she said.

"I'll do everything before I go. I promise."

"Plus, an eleven-year-old boy can't just ride off into the night in a limousine. Absolutely not."

I was so twisted inside I felt sick. Then I had the greatest brainstorm of my life.

"Mom," I said.

She had already started to walk away.

"You come, too."

XIX

The First Game

THE FIRST GAME was against the Cavaliers, and I knew it was going to be a stone cold annihilation by the Thunder. Rooster Oosterbaan was still hobbling around, but Fat Abs Pintcher had picked up the old veteran Artiste LaRue from the Heat to replace Rooster in the middle.

Fat Abs got Artiste, who was way over seven feet tall, for, like, nothing because the Heat thought he couldn't score a basket if you put the hoop under his nose and told him to drop the ball. Anyway, that's what Larry Wheeling told me he'd heard on the radio. The thing was, with the Thunder, Artiste LaRue didn't have to do anything, except stand like a tree and keep little guys from driving to the hole. Jasper Jasmine would take care of the scoring. My man.

And Selby O'Hara, the real pale, real quiet, great assist-giving old point guard for the Thunder, had suddenly started lighting it up. He had a three-point shot that was funky-looking like a kid's—you know kind of coming from the shoulder—but when he launched it, the whole crowd started going, "Ye-e-e-e-sssss!" even before it went in. He had thirty the other night, in a win over the Magic. Of course, Jasper Jasmine had thirty-eight. Sixty-eight points was pretty sweet from your two guards.

Mom had dressed up like we were going to Cinderella's ball, and in the limo she kept rubbing the seat and saying, "I just don't know about this. I just don't know." It had taken me a long time to talk her into coming. I told her how exciting it was and how she would get royal treatment. I didn't push. I didn't want her to say no. I just let it kind of hang there like this cool thing that would be fun. Before Dad left she would have been fired up to go to a big event like this. But nowadays she was nervous about everything.

When we got there, some Thunder people gave her flowers and led her to the fancy box, and as she went away, she was smiling and jabbering like crazy. She could be up and down like that. You just never knew.

They took me to a room near the Thunder's locker room, and I got to put on a white shirt with a thundercloud on it and my initials, RD, above the pocket. The team trainer told me what to do—just collect the balls, give guys water and chewing gum when they wanted it, give them towels, mop the floor if there was sweat on it, and mostly stay out of the way. There was another kid doing the same thing for the visiting team. And there were adults for the important stuff, like holding clipboards and charting stuff.

When the Thunder came out for warmups, I stood there gawking. Their shoes squeaked as they ran in a circle, and they were so tall and so awesome. I almost couldn't breathe.

Then somebody was bent over looking me right in the face.

"You gonna get us some balls or catch flies with your mouth?" the voice said.

It was Jasper Jasmine.

I got the balls out in a hurry.

After a couple minutes, Jasper Jasmine walked up to me again.

"How's it going Rob?" he said, turning to swish a long shot then getting the ball back from a teammate.

"Good," I said. "Thanks, Mr. Jasmine."

"Just do a good job. How's the fort?"

"Fine," I said. I think I was blushing.

"I may have to visit again," he said. "I miss Sol."

I nodded. "He misses you."

"Where's your mom?"

"How'd you know I brought her?"

"A hunch."

I pointed her out—about ten rows up in a box—and Jasper Jasmine waved. Mom waved back then put both hands over her mouth and blinked real fast. She was kind of wound up.

The Thunder toyed with the lousy Cavaliers, and Jasper Jasmine only scored twenty-four points because he came out of the game early. Ben G. Bancroft strolled down the bench and stood in front of Jasper, who was sitting on one of the cushioned Thunder chairs, a white towel over his shoulders, sweat beads on his face and neck. The coach kneeled down beside Jasper Jasmine, and they both watched the game for a while. I was right behind them on my chair with the raised seat so I could see.

They didn't say anything for the longest time. Then Ben G. Bancroft got up, dusted his knees, leaned over and whispered to Jasper, "The cigars are in."

Jasper Jasmine kept looking out at the floor. After a while he said, "Macanudos?"

"Cohibas, mostly," said Ben G. Bancroft.

Jasper nodded. His face never turned from the game. Ben G. Bancroft patted Jasper Jasmine on the shoulder and walked away.

After the game a TV reporter came sprinting out with his crew and jammed a microphone in front of Jasper Jasmine. The guy asked him the usual, and Jasper Jasmine was smooth as can be. Then he said something and pointed to me. The camera and its lights swung over to me and my pile of dirty towels. Jasper walked over and hoisted me by the shoulder until I was standing up. He put his arm around me and turned back to the camera guys, who had moved toward us.

"Our secret weapon," he said, pointing at me. "The amazing ball boy."

I looked straight into the camera. Like the moron I am.

XX

School

AT SCHOOL I WAS ALMOST A HERO. A lot of guys saw me on TV, and they were out of their minds.

"Rob, you are . . . you are . . . I don't know what you are," said Kenny Koski.

"Did he talk to you?" asked somebody else.

"Do you get to do it again?"

"Is he as tall as he looks?"

"How cool was it?"

"Can you take me?"

"Can you?"

I told the guys I had three more games but I couldn't take anybody. My mom had to come. They kept begging me, but there was nothing I could do.

When I walked down the hall between classes, I could see people talking about me. Some of them looked confused.

Some stared or looked once and moved along. But nobody was laughing at me. Not even the seventh-graders.

I went to practice. I'd gotten a notice from the doctor, who had examined my nose and head, and I was cleared to play again. My mom was still against it, and, in fact, she was having some problems again. She just wasn't handling things real well was the truth. She had pills to take, but they didn't always work. I saw her sitting in the kitchen, crying, the night before. It was like the Thunder game had almost never happened. But I didn't know why I couldn't go back to my fifth-grade team, if I was careful and not so wild and avoided getting hurt. Mom had just waved me away. "Do what you want," she said.

Chet "Chewy" Looey was back, and Coach Raltney wouldn't use me in scrimmages, just like old times. But that was okay. I did the drills, and I was racking the balls again. People didn't mind having me around.

The only guy who was making things rough was Vance Lester.

Ball boy, he started calling me. "Get the ball, boy," he'd say. "Fetch. Good ball boy."

He came up and said, "I'll bet Jasper Jasmine doesn't even know your name. Maybe he thinks it's Fetch."

"He's been to my house," I said.

"Right."

"He has."

"Sure."

"Honest, he has."

"But has your dad been to your house?"

"Shut up, Vance."

"Ha."

"Just shut up."

"Wanna make me, ball boy?"

I felt the old nothingness come over me again. Vance was bigger than me and such a good athlete. I wanted to hit him so hard. I wanted to do something big and strong and be so good at it and shut Vance up and make him know that there were guys like me who wanted to play more than anything but just didn't have everything going in the right order.

Vance looked at me and laughed.

"Where's Jasper Jasmine when you need him?" he said.

He dribbled away.

XXI

Game Two

MOM WENT WITH ME TO GAME TWO, but she seemed sad again. She looked nice in a green dress with matching shoes, but she didn't get as excited as before. The Thunder was playing the Pacers, and it was a much better game than the one against the Cavaliers. At least, it was a lot rougher.

There was a collision in the first quarter, between Artiste LaRue and the Pacers center, and both men fell down, so I had to run onto the floor with my mop and clean up the sweat. Usually, I just mopped under the basket, but this was out near center court. It was so bright and amazing out there, I felt like I was underneath the sun, on a beach. I could hear the ref telling the players to tone it down a little.

"Why don't you tone it *up*," Eduardo Jackson said, almost in the ref's ear.

"Careful," said the ref. "Careful."

Eduardo moved closer. "Let me kiss you, see if that makes you blow your whistle."

"A T's coming, Eduardo. I mean it."

"You ain't got the stones."

"Try me."

"You're a joke."

"That's it." The ref blew his whistle long and hard and signaled a technical foul on Eduardo Jackson, which set off even more complaining from Eduardo. I got off the floor just when the ref blew the second technical on Eduardo, and that was it for Eduardo because you only get two and then you're tossed. And Eduardo was tossed. Guards had to go with Eduardo to make sure he left the court. Beer cups and programs came flying out of the stands. I heard some coins go clinking across the wood. Somebody threw a golf ball. Eduardo got to the sidelines, and the crowd was roaring for him and booing the ref. Eduardo took off his jersey, swung it around his head, and threw it way into the stands. The crowd went even crazier.

Eduardo started to go into the tunnel, but he came back. He took off one shoe at a time and threw them into the stands. Then he tried to go back on court. The guards kept him off. But he still didn't leave. He waved to the crowd and blew kisses, and then, honest to god, he took off his trunks. He was wearing training shorts underneath, so he wasn't naked or anything, but it was pretty weird. The whole stadium went insane.

Eduardo threw the shorts over the heads of the guards and over the Pacers' bench toward the ref out on the floor. He pointed at the ref and screamed, and then finally he left.

Wow. I looked over at Jasper Jasmine, who had his arms crossed on his chest. He looked fairly annoyed.

The Pacers played a good game after that, but in the end the Thunder made a bunch of free throws, and Selby O'Hara dropped in a bomb before the buzzer and the Thunder won, ninety-two to eighty-seven. It was their tenth straight win at home, going back to last season, and things were definitely looking good.

As Jasper Jasmine was walking into the tunnel, I caught up with him. He had an easy thirty-two points and a bunch of steals.

"Do you smoke cigars?" I asked.

He stopped and looked at me. "It's the filthiest, nastiest, stupidest vice in the world," he said. "And if you ever pick up a cigar, I'll have you arrested. But since you asked, yes. But only after a win. Which is why I don't lose much."

XXII

The Visitor

"GIMME THE TIGHT WEAVE," yelled Mr. Raltney. "Three man. Like a braid."

We got in lines and did the full-court weaves, throwing the ball back and forth until the last man shot a lay-up. Then we came back. Of course, there were only two of us in the last group because of the numbers and naturally that was me and, as it turned out, Kenny Koski. Everybody else wove in and out, but we just went back and forth with the ball like two guys playing catch. It wasn't much fun that way, but I tried to throw the ball right where Kenny could catch it real easy. I made it a challenge.

"Rob," said Kenny after we finished a round, "You're breaking my fingers. Just pass it to me. I'm like two feet away.

"Sorry," I said.

I guess I was concentrating too hard on the follow-through. I daydreamed a little.

I thought about winter coming. I thought about my nose—which the doctor didn't set because, he said, it was just a hairline fracture—and how, when I looked in the mirror sometimes, my nose seemed to go to the left just a teensy bit. But maybe I was just looking at it too hard or my head was crooked. Mirrors are very strange things because words are backwards, and it seems possible to me that your whole face is not the way it really is but somehow backwards, too—or at least not the way it is in real life. I thought about Sol. He was doing okay for a salamander, which was a life that I tried to think about: Rob, you're a salamander. My, this rotten tree trunk looks nice. Nice leaves. Hey, here are some yummy worms. Whoa, dude, a cricket.

I was in my fort yesterday with the candles lit and I started reading the dictionary. I'd been reading it for a year or so, and a couple weeks ago, I finished *j*. I looked through *k* for a while, but I got stuck on *kaf*, which is the eleventh letter of the Hebrew alphabet. I started thinking about how that must be *k* for Hebrew people because *k* is the eleventh letter in English, and then I thought about letters and started wondering what an alphabet is and what I'd do if I was making one up. I'd get rid of cursive, that's for sure, and maybe capitals, and I'd have a letter that was like an *o*, but it would have curved lines through it, and that would be the letter basketball.

I skipped ahead and went through some *l*'s: *Lacy*. *Lag*. *Lemur*. *Ligature*. My mind was all over the place. *Loser*. There it was. *Loser*. One that loses. One that seems doomed to lose. Well, hello, Rob Denwood. How strange, because I was lucky enough to know the greatest man on Earth. Why would I still feel like this? That was me retrieving a ball at the sold-out

Thunder game, running across the floor over the purple-and-black thundercloud with the gold lightning bolts, and grabbing the wonderful ball and holding it and running it back and handing it to Jasper Jasmine. That was me. But I looked at that word. *Loser.* Pronounced *loo-zer.* Like lazer. Like lizard. Like loser.

"Hey, dipwad, get off the court."

It was Vance Lester. His voice startled me. My mind had been wandering, like I said. I guess they were getting ready to scrimmage. I looked at Vance, and he was looking at me the way he always does.

Well, I hadn't been paying attention, so I couldn't blame him or anyone else, for that matter, for getting on my case a little. I thought Vance was going to say something else nasty to me, but all of a sudden there was this strange look in his eyes. He was looking straight past me like he was looking at a skeleton. Beside him Billy McReynolds looked funny, too. Billy's mouth was open. I looked at Mr. Raltney, and he was, like, frozen, too, and looking in the same place that everybody else was now.

I turned around.

There by the door was a tall man in a beautiful business suit. I could see the diamond earring in his ear sparkle, even where I was. One of the guys shouted, and then another one did, and then somebody else almost, like, screamed. Then there was quiet.

"Jasper Jasmine," said Mr. Raltney.

Personally, I thought maybe Mr. Raltney was going to die.

Jasper Jasmine nodded.

So cool. So tall and calm. There was a guy next to Jasper Jasmine—or not really next to him, but back in the doorway—

and I recognized him from the stadium. His name was Leonard, and I knew that he was a policeman in regular clothes, like a bodyguard for Jasper Jasmine, to keep the weirdos away when the big crowds piled up on him. The man never said anything, and he walked along with Jasper a lot, sometimes following him right up to his car, which was parked under the stands down a tunnel, or stepping out to put his arm in front of excited people now and then, and his eyes just roamed around like Ping-Pong balls. Leonard stayed back in the doorway, and Jasper Jasmine took a couple more steps our way.

"Well," said Mr. Raltney. "Well."

Coach needed to get a grip on himself. He was almost shaking, and he had this, like, deranged grin on his face.

"Hi," said Mr. Raltney. "I'm Coach Raltney, and this is my fifth-grade team, and you're Jasper Jasmine."

Jasper stepped forward and shook Mr. Raltney's hand and said, "Yes, I am." Then he looked around.

He saw me and he winked. He said, "I know this is your team, Coach. I thought I'd just stop by on my way to the stadium and see some good ball players. And you got my man there, my main dude, Robby Denwood."

He walked over and said, "What's up, bud?" and I said, "Just the usual."

Mr. Raltney got all slobbery-mouthed, and after talking way too much, he asked Jasper Jasmine if Jasper could say a few words to the team.

"Oh, I don't have much to tell you," said Jasper Jasmine, looking at everybody. "Ben G. Bancroft always tells us to breathe deep and be in the moment, so I'll tell you that, too. Nothing beats hard work. Enjoy the game. Look at the back of the rim if your shot's short. Don't lose your temper. That's about it. Coach, you got things going pretty good on your own, so I'll just say good luck to you all."

He shook everybody's hand, and the kids were going, like, wow and laughing because they were shaking Jasper Jasmine's hand and it was so huge and, of course, he was famous. He got to me, and we did this funny forearm tap, then elbow, then shake thing he had taught me.

"This is the man right here," he said, looking around at everybody and tapping me on the head. "The man. See you at the game tomorrow Rob?"

I said, "Yes." Then Jasper Jasmine waved and went back off the floor and out the door, and the guys, as you can imagine, thought I was a pretty big deal.

I could see the bodyguard join in with Jasper Jasmine as he went down the hall.

Guys were jabbering like maniacs. Except for Vance Lester. He had his mouth shut.

XXIII

Game Three

MOM WASN'T FEELING GOOD, or at least that's what she said, and I believed her. She missed a day of work, and when I asked her if there was anything I could get her, she said no. She didn't have the flu or a cold or anything. She was blue, she said, and I didn't know exactly what she meant, but I knew it had to do with Dad and our house and money, and probably Lulu, and no doubt me being such a dope.

I asked her if she was coming to the game, and she said no. *Uh-oh.* I hoped she wasn't just upset about Eduardo Jackson acting crazy the other night. In the limo home she had been kind of quiet. Neither of us had mentioned the flying shorts.

I asked her if I could still go, and she said, "Whatever."

At least now she knew for sure I was telling the truth about everything with Jasper Jasmine. I'd told her how that night he drove me home, we had gone for a walk in the woods, and she didn't believe that at first. But then at the last game, Jasper had told her it was true. She still didn't know why a world-famous man like Jasper Jasmine would even notice I was alive, but then I didn't either, so what could I tell her?

"Well, who will come with me?" I asked.

"I have no idea," she said.

I had to think about this. This was big. Very big. Something hit me.

"How about Lulu?" I asked.

Mom had walked out of the kitchen and was lying on her bed. There was a glass of water and a box of tissues on the nightstand. Some magazines. The shades were already closed. She had her robe on from the morning and never changed.

"What?"

"How about if Lulu goes to the game with me?"

"Fine. Take Lulu."

I don't know why I said Lulu. It just came out after that little brainstorm I had, but now I had to get old screamer herself to go with her little brother to a thing that she knew nothing about. Basketball to Lulu was like hair curlers sort of are to me. Or that gross stuff she puts on her face at night.

I knocked on the door of Lulu's room and she yelled, "Go away, freakazoid."

So I told her the plan through the door.

I was amazed when she actually opened her door after a while and said okay But she said, "I'm only going if I don't have to take care of you and you don't touch me and I get free food and the place where I sit is special and I'm not bored."

I said, "Absolutely, no problem."

I told her the Thunder was playing the Clippers, and that meant nothing to her. She slammed the door in my face and,

I guess, started to get ready. I know the only reason she said yes was so she could go in the limo and act like a supermodel.

We got to the game early, as usual, and there were people to take Lulu to her box seat. They said she looked nice and all this other nonsense, and she liked that. I went past the guards, with my pass, and into the little room where I could change into my white Thunder shirt. The other kid was there, and he said hi. I said hi, and he said he was going out now, even though it was early, because Sasha Solkaitis was already warming up. Sasha Solkaitis was the Clippers' guard who could shoot like crazy. Against the Lakers last week, he took forty-two shots, more than anybody in the whole league this year. He's kind of a gunner.

I had my own open locker, with two hooks in it, and a bench to sit on. There wasn't a nameplate up above like the players have, but there was some white tape with DENWOOD on it, and it was overall very cool. I changed into my shirt and sat down. I could hear the usual pregame noises coming through the door. Workers yelling, carrying boxes of food around. Big guys rolling beer kegs. Security guys' radios making that crackly sound. Footsteps. Heels clicking. Sneakers running by. Every now and then a ball bouncing down the tile. Little golf carts zipping past. Somebody singing way off. The organ man practicing.

I could do this all the time, I started thinking. Just skip right through fifth grade and high school and college and be a pro player. Of course, I wasn't a pro player. I wasn't sure what I was. Eleven. A lucky guy. A loser. A ball boy who still hadn't played a second of real basketball, with his sister acting like the queen of England.

The door opened.

"Well, if it ain't my man, Robby."

Jasper Jasmine walked in fast and closed the door.

He had on his full sweat suit and brand-new shoes that had purple heels and gold lighting bolts down the sides.

"Hi, Mr. Jasmine," I said.

There was a knock at the door.

"Jasper," someone was yelling. "Jasper, can I get you to sign your autograph for my sergeant back at the desk?"

"I'm busy," yelled Jasper. "In a while." He shook his head.

"Do people ever leave you alone?" I asked.

He sat down in front of the locker next to mine.

"Not really. I'm like a doorknob. First thing they reach for."

"Kind of a pain, huh?" I said.

"Comes with the territory, my friend."

He looked at me. Checked me out.

"You doing okay?"

I nodded.

"Playing any?"

"After you came, Mr. Raltney let me scrimmage on the second team during practice. I got in again yesterday."

"Did you slam any?"

"Oh yeah. I'm, like, monster jammin' all the time."

We both laughed.

"Well, I just stopped by to ask you one thing," he said.

"What's that?"

"How's my buddy Solomon doing?"

Before I had a chance to answer, the door opened again and Eduardo Jackson came flying in carrying a clothes bag. He was wearing jeans and a T-shirt, but he looked strange, and when he looked at Jasper Jasmine and then at me I realized he had makeup on, with blue on his eyelids and big, long eyelashes.

He didn't say anything. He only kind of grunted at Jasper Jasmine, then he hung the bag up in a locker across the room and took the plastic wrap off. What was hanging there was a dress.

"Oh Lord," said Jasper Jasmine. "No, you don't."

Eduardo had another small bag with him, and he set it on the bench.

"You aren't even supposed to be here, Eduardo," said Jasper.

"Like you care."

"What are you doing? You're suspended. You aren't even supposed to be in the building."

"Eduardo Jackson is suspended. Not Eduinna Jackson."

"No," said Jasper. "Come on. You can't be serious."

"Chill, J. J. I'm not playing. I'm just gonna be in the stands, like a fan."

"No. Don't. Please."

Eduardo took the dress into the shower room, and in a second, Jasper Jasmine followed. I could hear some loud talking, mostly from Jasper. Then Eduardo was yelling. Back and forth.

I heard Eduardo laughing real hard.

"I mean, you cannot hide this kind of beauty," he said.

In a minute, this really tall lady came out, wearing a dress. It was Eduardo and it wasn't.

"They'll suspend you till the playoffs," said Jasper Jasmine, following right behind. "They'll send you to the shrink again."

"*They*," said Eduardo. "*They* are not gonna know."

He sat down and dumped out the small bag. He put on some ladies' slippers and picked up this brown curly thing and walked into the shower area. He came back, and he had a wig on. He looked in the little mirror next to the door, and he straightened the wig. It looked like he had a dog on his head.

"Don't," said Jasper Jasmine.

Eduardo turned and winked at both of us.

"Would either of you like to dance?" he said.

Jasper hung his head.

"Later, boys," Eduardo said. Then he was out the door.

Jasper Jasmine didn't move for a while. I couldn't help it—I ran to the door and looked out, and there down the hall went Eduardo Jackson, with his shoulders looking huge and he was holding hands with that famous lady, who I think was his girlfriend. He was wearing the dress, and I saw this one cop almost fall on the floor when they went by.

I closed the door.

Jasper Jasmine was sitting and leaning against the wall. Now he was looking at the ceiling.

"No matter what," he said. "No matter what."

I didn't know what he was talking about.

"No matter what. Life is not simple."

"You're right," I said. "You're absolutely right."

* * *

During the game, I kept looking for Eduardo in the stands but couldn't find him. I wondered if he even stayed at the Thunder Dome. Or maybe he hid in the wives' room, which is across from the players' locker and has a bar in it and a TV and stuff.

The game was pretty bad, at least for the Thunder. Jake Van Beeker played a lot because Eduardo was suspended. He

111

tried hard, but he couldn't stop the Clippers' power forwards and he couldn't get many rebounds the way he usually does. Shantee Williams also played for the Thunder, but he is slow and always seems to get his shots blocked at the wrong time. Jasper Jasmine, I think, took it personally that Sasha Solkaitis just shoots whenever he feels like it. Jasper held Solkaitis to only eighteen shots, and just seven went in. But Jasper couldn't do it all himself, and the Thunder lost for the first time in two weeks. The announcer made a big deal before the game about the Thunder being undefeated at home this season, but he didn't say anything about that afterward.

In the limo on the way home, I started to fall asleep, but Lulu wouldn't let me. She wanted to tell me all about the fancy food she got in her box seat and how the people thought she was so cute and so unique and blah-blah-blah. She said she sat next to the most incredible stars and just three seats behind her this famous actress lady who is in all these commercials was there. And the actress was sitting with the tallest, ugliest woman Lulu had ever seen.

I was dead tired, but now I kind of perked up.

"How ugly?" I asked.

"Oh my god," said Lulu, "she looked like she had a dog on her head."

XXIV

The Fort

THE LEAVES FELL when the wind picked up, and the way they fell was awesome. It depended what kind of tree you were under, but if it was a maple with big fat leaves, you could chase those leaves or just choose one in the sky and then follow it and run and catch it before it hit the ground. It wasn't easy, but you could do it. It helped me to make up something like, If I don't get this leaf before it lands on the grass, my head will explode. That made it even more intense.

I was actually standing, looking up in the sky, when Jasper Jasmine pulled into my driveway. He had a different car than the other times. This one was a freaked-out light blue Humvee. It was almost like a tank. It was sparkling clean and wide as a house, and the glass was all tinted and the license plate said 7 Heven.

I couldn't believe he was here again, but it was Saturday, and the next game wasn't until tomorrow, and somehow it seemed almost normal to me.

"Hi, Robby," said Jasper Jasmine, as he got out of the huge car. I jumped back for a second, because when Jasper opened the door I saw there was another guy in there.

"I brought a friend."

"I see him," I said.

"No," Jasper said, chuckling. "That's Leonard, my guard. You've seen him before."

"Oh, yeah," I said. The guy, Leonard, never said anything. His eyeballs just went around.

"No," said Jasper. "Here's my friend."

He walked to the passenger's side of the car and opened the door. Then he pulled out about the cutest little boy I'd ever seen.

"Meet my son, Anthony," he said.

The little kid just stared at me, then looked all around.

"Anthony," said Jasper Jasmine, "this is my friend, Robby Denwood."

The boy was just a toddler kind of kid, way before preschool, one of those droolers who could cry like crazy if you gave them a chance. But his eyes were huge and he was smiling and he held on to his dad like a koala bear hanging onto a tree.

I gave Anthony a little tickle on his side, and he giggled and pulled his shoulders up.

"Did you know koala bears live in eucalyptus trees?" I said to him. "And they eat eucalypus leaves? That's all they do. And their fur smells just like cough drops because of it."

The Fort

I tickled Anthony again. Then I had an idea.

"Hey," I said, "how would you like to see something neat in the woods?"

The little guy didn't know what I was talking about, and he buried his face in his dad's shirt, but Jasper Jasmine said to me, "I was hoping we could do that."

The three of us went around back, and I didn't worry about anybody seeing us because nobody was home at my house. And I didn't think anybody would freak over the Humvee just yet. Plus, Leonard could take care of any little kid who rode up or whatever. *Just pull the gun, Leonard,* I thought. *That will clear the driveway.* I showed the way to get onto my path, which is sort of there but sort of not. We went slow and we stopped to look at the leaves and some mushrooms. I even showed Anthony where a squirrel nest was way up high and a place where a deer had chewed the bark off a balsam tree.

Clouds were flying overhead, and the sun came and went. The colors around us changed back and forth, and the wind sent leaves dropping down through the trees. When we got to the clearing, Jasper put Anthony down and the boy ran around in circles saying, "Yeah, yeah, yeah." I laughed because he was so funny.

"Hey, Anthony," I said.

He looked at me.

"Look what's over here."

He walked over toward me, and then I lifted the canvas door to my fort. I turned back to him and made my eyes real big, and I said, "What is this?"

"Dada," he said, and he looked back at Jasper.

"What is it, Anthony?" Jasper said. "Is that a fort?"

The little boy looked inside. Then he looked at his dad. He nodded his head up and down.

"Want to go in?" I said. "Let's all go in, okay?"

I put the flap over a limb and went in first. Then Anthony came in and sat on my lap. Then Jasper Jasmine got as small as he could and crunched his way inside.

Anthony pointed out at the dead tree and said, "Horsey."

"No, that's a tree," I said. "Go sit with daddy for a second, little guy."

Then I got the matches and lit the candles.

"No, no, don't touch," I told Anthony. "Those are hot."

The candles lit up the back of the fort and I showed Anthony where Flossie was in her web. Then I pulled Sol out of his terrarium.

"You can pet him," I said. "He's nice."

"Doggie," said Anthony.

"No, he's a salamander. Can you say salamander?"

Anthony said, "Sammer."

"Very good," I said.

We sat there for a while, and the wind stopped, and then very softly it started to rain. It wasn't a big storm, just a nice steady rain that made everything sound good and comfortable. I was going to close the door, but it was better being able to look out at the forest and hear the rain and see the little streams and puddles it made and not get wet. I knew my fort would stay dry, because I'd been in it in some big rains, and even sleet. There were times I'd slept in it and didn't ever want to leave.

"Do you like this?" Jasper Jasmine asked me. Anthony was playing with the soldiers and sitting between the two of us.

"Yes," I said.

"I do, too," said Jasper.

I laughed.

"You have a house that's ten thousand times cooler than this," I said. "I've seen it on ESPN."

"But it's not like this."

"But you're not a kid."

"Sometimes I wouldn't mind being one, Robby. It's easy to feel like a prisoner."

"Do you think Sol is a prisoner?"

"No. He's got you making his life easy."

We watched the rain come down and then slowly it stopped.

"We visitors better be leaving," said Jasper. "Mrs. Jasmine will be expecting her men pretty soon."

We crawled out, and it wasn't as dry in the clearing as I'd thought. I went over to a tree and grabbed a branch that was up as high as I could reach, then bent it around in a circle and hooked it together so that it stayed like that. I ducked back into the fort and got my little ball, and I said to Jasper, "Okay, me and Anthony against you in tree ball."

I ran a couple steps with the ball. I was going to jump, but my feet slid out from under me and—*splat*—I landed on my back, in a puddle.

Anthony started laughing, then he just dove into a puddle and grabbed a glob of mud in each hand.

"Oh, no," said Jasper Jasmine. But then he dropped to his knees and I grabbed the ball and handed it to Anthony and said, "Dribble it, dribble it! Now pass it!" The little kid rolled the ball back to me, and I picked it up and dove over the top of Jasper Jasmine, then dunked the ball through the limb. The branch went *twang* and flipped up in the air, and a couple twigs shot off, and then we were all slopping around in the slop.

It was hysterical. Every time Jasper Jasmine took a shot from his knees, I swatted it away, and Anthony ran and picked the ball up. Anthony climbed up on my shoulders, and I became the horse and he was the rider. When he jammed the ball through the tree limb hoop, he thought that was about the funniest thing that ever happened.

Boy, we were a mess.

I figured I'd use the hose in the backyard to clean myself up before Mom knew what was happening, but I didn't know what Jasper was going to do. Maybe Leonard could give him some cop clothes. Jasper and Anthony in that Humvee were going to be a problem. But I didn't care. Jasper had never beaten me at any game of basketball.

"You are weak," I told Jasper as I dunked on him. "Your game is weak. Your game is so small I can't see it."

Then he grabbed my ankle, and I went splattering into the mud one more time.

XXV

Game Four

NOBODY WENT WITH ME to the game on Sunday afternoon against the Mavericks. Lulu was somewhere else, and Mom said she was tired and basketball was totally ignorant and she didn't know why she went the other times.

I needed to go, so I thought about the guys at school. But for some reason I didn't want any of them coming along. It was like this was mine, and all they could do was ruin it. Who else? There wasn't anybody. What about Kathy? I don't know. It was a longshot. All she knew about basketball was what I'd told her. A girl. I still felt bad about leaving her at the mall.

I got her number out of the school directory, and her father answered when I called.

"Can I talk to Kathy, please?" I said.

"She's at her grandmother's for the afternoon. Who's calling?"

"It's Robby. I'm in her class."

"Can I give her a message?"

"Well, I wondered if she wanted to go to a Thunder game. I have a limo."

"When is the game?"

"Two-thirty."

"What day?"

"Today."

"That's in two hours."

"I know. The limo's here."

Mr. Amblee laughed. "I'll certainly tell Kathy when she returns with her mother. But it's too late for today. Maybe another time. You're not driving that limo, are you?"

"Oh no, I'm only eleven. Mr. Harrison, the driver, drives it."

"Okay, Robby. Have a good time."

So I rode alone. When the limo pulled up to the gate at the Thunder Dome, some kids were outside and they gathered around the door to see who was going to get out.

They had on dirty clothes and they looked inside the car to see who else was getting out. When they saw it was only me, they started saying things.

"Hey, rich boy, gimme some money."

"Yo, man, take me for a ride."

"Come on, gimme a dollar."

I went right on through the employees' door. Those kids didn't have any idea who I was. It bothered me because I wasn't really the person they thought I was. But how could anybody know who you were if you acted one way but really were another?

Inside the stadium there was a lot of stuff happening in that nervous way it happens before big games. Players were walking down the halls in their street clothes. Cops were everywhere.

Some rock-and-roll guys with guitars were practicing a song in the corner even though their guitars weren't plugged into anything. Two Japanese TV crews were yelling at each other, and this other TV man was standing in front of his camera crew with a bright light on him, talking in Spanish, I think, or French, and standing where everybody had to walk around him. Every now and then, he'd open a little mirror thing and put powder on his nose and rub his teeth with his tongue. I could see why the TV guys annoyed the heck out of Jasper Jasmine.

Out on the floor two other crews were filming their TV person. Both these people were talking in English, and I heard one lady say, "We'll show you the footage now of what is apparently Eduardo Jackson in disguise at last Thursday's Clippers game. There. He allegedly is the woman in the wig and blue dress next to actress Destiny Dee. Jackson denies it was him, and for now the Commissioner has no plans to take action. Jackson is expected back in the starting lineup tonight—as a man. From the Thunder Dome, I'm . . ."

I went into my changing room and put on my white shirt. I got some paper towels from the bathroom area and wetted them in the sink, then wiped all the mud off my basketball shoes. They were still a little grungy from our rain game yesterday.

The Thunder had begun stretching at their end of the floor, and then they started running some lay-up drills. It always amazed me how even little guys like Freon Mack and Muhammed El-Mullah could get their hands way above the rim. Jasper Jasmine didn't even bother dunking usually but just dropped the ball in from about three feet over the hole. Eduardo Jackson was in the lay-up line, but he would dribble

in and then not even shoot, just set the ball on the floor and
look out at the people coming into the arena like he was
bored. At least I think that's how he was looking. But I
couldn't see for sure because he was wearing sunglasses.

After a few minutes big old Rooster Oosterbaan came out
and got in the line, and that was great because he looked
pretty much healed from his injury. Boy, the Thunder needed
his big butt in the middle. I got busy then running around,
handing guys towels and retrieving balls and getting tape
rolls for their fingers. Lonnie Patterson wanted some gum
from his locker, so I had to run in and get that. Jake Van
Beeker wanted a red rubber band to go with the blue one on
his wrist, so I ran all the way to the secretary's office to get
him one. Then Eduardo Jackson came over and said, "Kid,
get my headphones; they're in my bag in the meeting room."
I could see myself reflected twice in his sunglasses.

Oh man, I had to take the elevator up a floor and go past
two guards and finally ask the security man to unlock the
door, and he watched me while I found the headphones in
Eduardo's bag. There were about a million CDs in the bag,
too, and lipstick and boxes of raisins and even a stuffed dog.
I went flying back down to the floor and ran up to Eduardo
and handed him the earphones. He took them and didn't say
a thing. He plugged the headset into a CD player clipped to
his waistband. Then, when I was walking away he said, "Yo."
I turned around and walked back, and he reached in the side
of his trunks and pulled out a giant wad of bills inside a clip.
He peeled off a twenty and gave it to me. "Keep it real," he
said. Then he wandered off to the scorers' table, moved some
books and papers, and lay down.

There was what they call tension in the air because this was a big game for the Thunder. The Thunder had lost at home for the first time in about a thousand years, and if they lost this game they would be almost .500 for the season, which for them was terrible. Four and three. You can't win the NBA title like that.

Jasper Jasmine came over to me as the players were getting ready to stand in line for the National Anthem and said, "You know why I'm irritable don't you?"

I shook my head no.

"Because I haven't had a cigar in five days."

While we stood there I looked at him and wondered if he felt safe. So many people always around him. People looking at him. People expecting stuff from him. And the world was kind of scary these days. He had that one bodyguard, Leonard, and now he had another one with him, too, a mean-looking man with a little radio earphone in his ear, and sideburns and long greasy black hair. Sometimes there were even three bodyguards with Jasper. They would walk around him as he moved through the arena or went to his car. Always looking around and stopping people from getting too close. Sometimes I would see all of them on TV, when the sports came on and Jasper Jasmine was making an appearance at a big event, or maybe he was getting out of his plane that flew him places.

Ben G. Bancroft gathered the starting five around him—Jasper Jasmine, Eduardo Jackson, Rooster Oosterbaan, Selby O'Hara, Lonnie Patterson—and drew Xs and Os on a small board with his special pen. Eduardo still had on his sunglasses, and now he had a toothpick in the corner of his mouth. He wasn't paying any attention. He was trotting in place, looking at the ceiling and singing to himself.

I was right there because I needed to grab the towels the players had, and I listened to Ben G. Bancroft talk. He was almost yelling because there was so much noise in the building, what with people getting fired up and a Rolling Stones song blasting out of the PA system and guys walking around on the floor shooting T-shirts into the upper deck out of their air bazookas.

"We know the Mavs are in first place in the west," said Ben G. Bancroft. "But we own the east. The east is ours. This is where it starts. No room for slack. No room for disruptive thoughts. If Lamar or Farrington gets hot on the perimeter, we double on the spot. Clamp down like the steel glove. Look into your hearts and be peaceful. Be fierce. Be in the moment."

Ben G. Bancroft looked down at the Mavericks' bench. Coach Gino Costello was looking back, and he smiled and mouthed the words *good luck*. Gino was short and had puffy hair and a shiny suit and a bright yellow tie that matched the yellow handkerchief in his suit pocket. Ben G. Bancroft smiled, too, and mouthed the words *good luck* back to Gino. Then he turned back to the huddle. His smile was gone.

"We need this win," Ben G. said. He looked at Jasper Jasmine. Sweat was trickling down Jasper's forehead.

"And Gino Costello," said Ben G. Bancroft looking right at Jasper, "I hate that phony little weasel. Let's go!"

The Thunder started out slowly, but that was mostly because of Rooster, who was having a hard time with the Mavs' really quick and skinny center, Wolfgang Schmick. Schmick took Rooster way outside and kept him from the middle of things. Then Schmick hit a couple three-pointers, and old Rooster didn't know what to do.

Ben G. Bancroft called a time-out and set up a switch so that Lonnie Patterson would take Schmick whenever he went outside, and Rooster would float in a zone around the lane. It worked, and Rooster got a dunk on offense—a Rooster Egg is what they they call it in the papers—and that seemed to settle him down. All the fans made that noise—*cock-a-doodle-doo!*—they make when Rooster does something good.

But mostly Jasper Jasmine was, like, on a mission. After a few minutes he started shooting and he couldn't miss. After he scored over Isaiah Farrington, the Mavs player who was covering him, he backpedaled down the floor, looking right at Farrington, saying, "You can't and you won't. Not now, not ever."

Jasmine took a lob from O'Hara and was so high above the rim, he almost hit his face on the backboard when he dunked. The Mavs started fouling Jasper, but that didn't do anything except put him on the line, and he was just as hot there. He had twenty-three points at the half and the Thunder were up fifty-four to forty-seven.

On the way into the locker room, the Thunder Cloud blimp that is remote controlled and flies around the inside of the stadium came down low over the players. All the players kept going into the tunnel and on to the locker room except for Eduardo Jackson, who stood and looked at the blimp as it slowly moved around. It's about the size of a fat canoe, and it's gray and blue, like a cloud, and when it got above Eduardo's head again, he took his towel, rolled it tight, and made a rat-tail out of it. Then he snapped the towel hard up in the air, and the tip hit the blimp with a *whap*, and ripped out a little piece of the covering, which went sailing off.

Gas or whatever was inside the blimp squealed out, and the blimp started shooting around in circles. The little plastic propeller that moved it didn't do anything now. The blimp went straight up almost to the top of the arena, then rolled like a log in water. Then it went straight down into the crowd, and people started punching it until it went back in the air. But it was half deflated and finally it drifted out over the court and slowly drooped over the frame that holds up the near basket and sort of, like, died.

Eduardo Jackson chuckled and walked on into the locker room. I stayed on the bench and folded clean towels and made sure the cups were straight on the watercooler table. Out of the corner of my eye I watched some maintenance men climb a ladder and get the blimp off the basket and fold it up like a tablecloth.

In the second half, the Thunder built the lead up to ten points, then fourteen. But when Jasper Jasmine came out to rest, the Mavericks scored nine points real fast, and then Delta Lamar got fouled on a three and made all three of his free throws. All of a sudden the game was close. I gave Jasper some Gatorade on the bench, and he drank it as fast as he could, then he squashed the cup and threw it hard on the floor. He got up and walked past Ben G. Bancroft, said a swear word, and walked straight to the scorers' table, and said, "I'm in."

He was still on fire, and he made his thirty-fifth point on a sweet fallaway, and the Thunder was back up by eight. The Mavericks called a time-out.

On our bench Ben G. Bancroft didn't even get up. He sat almost not moving. He looked calm. Finally he said something. "Figure it out."

That's all he said. "Figure it out."

Well, then Jasper grabbed his teammates one at a time and said something I couldn't hear. He looked pretty serious, though. He just nodded at Eduardo Jackson and didn't say anything to him. But they looked at each other.

Down at the Mavericks end, Gino Costello was putting Garth Stenko and Lou Hermans in for two of the starters. Garth and Lou were muscle guys who mostly played defense and fouled a lot. Stenko had a tattoo of a shotgun on his neck. Hermans did pro wrestling during the off-season. Costello looked down at the Thunder, and then his team made a circle around him.

XXVI  The Foul

THE ELECTRIC COMPANY DANCERS were flying around, kicking their legs, doing their fake cheer things. Over the PA came screeching rock music, and the big scoreboard flashed a sign saying, LOUDER! Fans were jumping up and down, and it was very intense.

Then, all of a sudden things went bad. Rooster fouled out, and Lonnie Patterson lost the ball out of bounds twice. The Mavericks tied the game, then went ahead on Delta Lamar's baseline jumper.

But Jasper Jasmine made two fadeaways and drew a nasty hack from Stenko. Eduardo Jackson went up to Stenko and put his face in Stenko's face after the foul and started talking. Spit was flying out of Eduardo's mouth. A vein on his forehead looked like a snake. Any second there was going to be a fight. But Jasper yanked Eduardo away. The TV people had been saying that if Eduardo got thrown out of another game, he could be suspended for a long time by the league. Jasper pulled Eduardo all the way to half-court and made him quiet down.

The game went back and forth, and when I looked at the scoreboard, I saw that Jasper Jasmine had forty-seven points. It was the fourth quarter, and he had made the last eight points for the Thunder, including four free throws because he kept getting smacked.

Then something happened. L. C. Quitman blocked a lay-up by Isaiah Farrington, and Jasper Jasmine had already snuck away and was running up the sideline the other direction. L. C. threw the ball to Selby O'Hara, who threw a long high pass to Jasper.

Jasper grabbed the ball out of the air like a football wide receiver and dribbled once, then twice. Then he crouched like a panther and he went up into the air from the side almost as far out as the free-throw line. There was nobody in front of him, and it seemed time just stopped. People were, like, stuck with their mouths open. The sound was gone. Nothing moved except Jasper, who floated so slow, so slow, way high up through the sky, one arm at his side and the other above his head, holding the orange ball as he moved toward the rim. He looked almost like an angel with no wings.

But Lou Hermans was running straight down the middle of the court as fast as he could, and I could see what was going to happen before it did. Time started again, and Hermans hit Jasper Jasmine in the legs from behind so hard, just as Jasper was slamming the ball down. The ball hit the back of the rim and shot straight up nearly to the scoreboard. Jasper Jasmine went flying sideways almost as high as the net, and when he hit the court his head bounced and his left arm and elbow got mashed underneath him.

It seemed like the whole arena sucked in its breath. The ref signaled a flagrant foul and made a T sign and instantly threw Hermans out of the game. If Hermans hadn't gotten off the floor as fast as he did and into the tunnel, with the cops around, I think the crowd might have killed him.

But there was Jasper Jasmine lying on the wood, not moving. His eyes were closed and he was holding his left elbow with his right hand. There were doctors around him, and the trainer and his teammates and Ben G. Bancroft, and even a couple TV camera guys came sneaking out. Leonard, the bodyguard, was there and he looked at the TV guys and said, "Get out of here, you rubbernecking scum." It was the first time I'd heard him speak.

Time went by, and still Jasper didn't get up. The refs cleared all the extra people off the floor, and then they waved for the players to go back to their benches. The announcer told everyone to stop throwing things at the Mavs bench and to remember good sportsmanship—and don't forget the police will arrest all lawbreakers.

I went out with my mop and began cleaning up the sweat that had gone all over the floor when Jasper Jasmine skidded to a stop. I mopped all around, and then I got close to him and I looked at him. The trainer was putting ice on Jasper's forehead, and one of the doctors was asking him if he could bend his arm, if he could feel anything bad in his elbow.

Jasper looked groggy like he'd been napping. He had his eyes shut again. And then he opened them, and he was looking at me. He was staring. I felt so bad for him, I said, "You can do it, Mr. Jasmine."

He closed his eyes and smiled, and then he said, "Not tonight."

Oh, I didn't want him to be hurt. I didn't want him to go out of the game. I didn't want any of this.

"Use what you have," I said.

"What?" he said. "Is somebody talking?"

"Sonny, get out of here," one of the doctors said to me. "Scram."

I looked at Jasper as I backed up.

"Use what you have," I said again.

This time Jasper shook his head, and I swear, he laughed.

"You're nuts," he said. "Who tells you this junk?"

They got Jasper Jasmine up finally, and two Thunder benchwarmers helped him slowly walk off the court and out of sight down the tunnel. The crowd screamed and booed and yelled out horrible stuff, and like I said, if Lou Hermans had been there he would have been in trouble.

The game started again, with O'Hara shooting and making all of Jasper's free throws. The Thunder got a one-point lead because of that, but real fast the Mavericks tied it up again. Every time the Mavericks had the ball, the whole building shook with *boos*. But the Thunder seemed confused and didn't know what to do on offense. During a break, the announcer said that Jasper Jasmine apparently had a minor concussion and bone chips in his left elbow and was being taken to the hospital for further tests. He would not be back tonight.

I looked at Ben G., who put his head in his hands and stared at the floor.

There were three minutes left in the game and the Mavericks were ahead by two when I noticed a wave of strange noise or a rumble with some screams start to come out of the stands. I couldn't tell what it was. It was kind of scary, and I wondered if something terrible was happening. It started at one side of the stadium, and then it fast moved around. People were pointing, and then they were screaming. Then the people next to them were screaming even louder and jumping and hitting each other, and I realized they were screaming at some policemen and Thunder security guys who were leading somebody or something toward the Thunder bench. The Thunder players stood up, and I saw them point and yell, too. I looked between the police and finally I saw what was happening.

Jasper Jasmine was walking back onto the floor.

Jasper was still in his uniform, but he had a bandage on his forehead and his left arm was hanging at his side, wrapped from his forearm to his biceps in tape. The arm wasn't straight, but it was pretty obvious it wouldn't bend much either. The Thunder called time-out. The noise was way past noise.

Ben G. Bancroft was out of his seat, and he had both his arms on Jasper's shoulders. He whispered something in Jasper's ear. I got up right next to them, being as small as I could be. I needed to hear. Ben G. Bancroft was a former player, and he was almost the same height as Jasper. Maybe even taller. Their faces were only inches apart.

"You don't have to do this," he said.

Jasper Jasmine stared at the coach and nodded.

"You're right," he said.

They looked at each other.

The Foul

Jasper Jasmine said, "But I need a cigar."

Jasper checked into the game, and it was the most amazing thing I've ever seen. He couldn't use his left arm like normal, and so he dribbled with it almost straight. He took jump shots that started way in front of him and ended up almost one-handed. His whole shot had changed, but when he let the ball go, it was the same as always. His arm didn't matter. On defense he was everywhere.

The Mavericks seemed scared to death of him. He couldn't be stopped. He finished with fifty-eight points, and the Thunder won by fifteen.

I didn't even try to go into the Thunder locker room afterward. I went into my room, which I could barely get to because of all the people and lights and guards in the hallway. Tonight there were even some men in those camouflage uniforms, with guns over their shoulders. It was like we were in the king's palace or something. I changed my shirt and sat on my bench. I could hear the noise through the walls. I knew the limousine would wait for me because you can't leave a kid at a place like this. I folded my Thunder shirt, which they said I could keep, and set it on my lap. Then I started crying.

I couldn't even tell you why I was crying. I just was.

Almost everyone was gone, and a guard looked in the room and said, "Closing time." I used a towel and wiped my face and looked in the mirror. "Knock it off," I said.

I grabbed my little duffel bag, and when I got into the limo, I unzipped it to put my Thunder shirt inside. There was an envelope in the bag.

It was sealed and on the front it said, *To Robby*, and below that: *From J. J.*

I asked Mr. Harrison, the driver, if it was okay if I turned on the reading light, and he said, "Sure." I flipped the switch, and a yellow circle of light appeared on the seat. I opened the envelope.

XXVII

The Letter

Dear Robby—

Sure has been good hanging with you. We have to leave now on our road trip, and we won't be back for two and a half weeks. They'll have new kids working as ball boys after that, but they'll never have another one like you. I'm writing this before the game because I may not get to see you afterward, especially if Eduardo gets in disguise again or there are too many reporters around. (Aren't there always?) I hope you have benefited from our time together as much as I have. By the way, Anthony sends his regards. Both of us love your fort, you know. Robby, life is tough, even my life. Don't give up, my friend. You're as special in your way as I am in mine.

Your pal—Jasper

PS—I found Eli, and I'm going to visit him on our West Coast trip.

XXVIII

The Fort

IT'S WARM TONIGHT. I mean it's warmer than it has been for a couple days, so it's a good time to be in the woods. The moon is so bright that I'm not going to have to turn on my flashlight for a while.

What I'm thinking right now is that the path is a stream and I'm walking on water. I'm a trout dancing on its tail. I'm a dragonfly.

Down I go past the balsam tree and all the other places I know really well. I like this walk almost as much as I like getting where I'm going. Already I miss the fun of the Thunder games and being with Jasper Jasmine, but I knew it was going to end even if I didn't want it to. The circus comes to the Thunder Dome every year at this time, and the team has to leave town until the circus finally packs up. Jasper told me that when they get back, the big hallways in the Thunder Dome smell like elephant poop for weeks.

The Fort

I've been thinking about a lot of things lately. And that's good. You're never too young to think about your future. I'm going to finish the year with my basketball team, but I'm not sure about after that. I might do something else.

Even in the dark I know that this is the oak tree where I turn left. I see the old log across the clearing, and I walk up to it and then to where it goes into the hill and I lift the door to my fort. I turn the flashlight on now because it's black inside.

"Aha, I caught you men sleeping," I say.

Sir, the sentry reported you and said you were a friendly.

"At ease. He is correct."

Orders, sir?

"Cover the flanks. Watch for trip wires. Vigilance."

Sir!

I look in the corner for Flossie, but she isn't there. Her web is kind of ragged, but there are a couple of egg sacs near the top. Maybe those are going to hatch next spring. Maybe they're old. Well, the fort isn't a bad place for a spider, and Flossie can stay or go. Whatever she wants.

But not Sol. He's here in his terrarium and he squirms when I pick him up. I had the flashlight under one arm, so I could reach in and get him, but I don't need the flashlight now. I turn it off. I walk out of the fort and put the flap down. Sol shines in the moonlight.

We float over the stream, walking on the water, dancing like dragonflies, and I find a nice spot near a grassy place, and I put Sol at the edge of some leaves and rotten wood. He glides off with his stumpy legs, and my eyes can see him slowly disappear. He is there and then he isn't, and I wonder if there is a word for that second when something changes like that.

I back up, and then I walk into the clearing. The moonlight is coming through the trees. It's silvery where it lights up the leaves on the way down. I can see the moon from here—it's a full moon and round like a basketball. Except the moon isn't totally full, but has a dent on one side like a ball that's a little flat and isn't perfect. But that's okay. It really is.